NURSERY
CRIMES

NURSERY CRIMES

Ayelet Waldman

BERKLEY PRIME CRIME, NEW YORK

NURSERY CRIMES

A Berkley Prime Crime Book
Published by The Berkley Publishing Group,
a division of Penguin Putnam Inc.,
375 Hudson Street
New York, New York 10014

The Penguin Putnam Inc. World Wide Web site address is
http://www.penguinputnam.com

First edition: June 2000

Library of Congress Cataloging-in-Publication Data

Waldman, Ayelet.
  Nursery crimes / by Ayelete Waldman.
    p. cm.
  ISBN 0-425-17469-7
  I. Title.

PS3573.A42124 L58 2000
813'.54—dc 21   99-046909

For Michael

NURSERY
CRIMES

One

I'M not sure whose fault it was, Ruby's or mine, that we didn't get in. Let's just say neither of us aced the admissions interview. I knew we were in trouble as soon as Ruby woke me up, at 6:00 A.M., with a scowl as black as the cowboy boots she had insisted on wearing to bed the night before. She refused to let me comb the left half of her hair, so I ended up walking out of the house holding the hand of a tiny little carny sideshow attraction: a half adorable, beribboned angel, half street urchin from hell. The effect was dramatized further by her chosen attire: Superman T-shirt, magenta miniskirt, and bright yellow clogs. She was impervious to my pleas, and seemed uninterested in my explanation of how not going to the right preschool would preclude Harvard, Swarthmore, or any other decent college. She'd end up at Slippery Rock State, like her dad. Even if she hadn't been two and a half years old, this would likely have made little impression on her. Her un-Ivied father made about ten times as much money as her thickly Ivied mother, and had an infinitely more satisfying career as a screenwriter than mine had been as a public defender.

By the time we got into the car, we were all three, Mama, Daddy, and Baby, in matching moods. Bad. Really, really bad. Peter was irritated because he'd had to get up before eleven. Ruby was irritated because I had turned off *The Big Comfy Couch* and forced her to eat some Cheerios and get out of the house. I was irritated at Ruby for being such a stubborn little brat, at Peter for failing to help me get her ready for the interview, and at myself for having gained fifty-five pounds in the first thirty-two weeks of my second pregnancy. I'd already outgrown most of my maternity clothes, and the only thing I could fit into was an old, dusty-black smock that I had worn to shreds when I was pregnant with the tiny Hell's Angel herself.

As we drove up Santa Monica Boulevard I desperately tried to give Ruby some last-minute admissions hints.

"Listen, Peach Fuzz, it's really important that you try to be sweet today, okay?"

"No."

"Yes. Yes. It is. You have to try to share with other kids. Don't grab toys or fight. Okay?"

"No."

"Yes. Hey, I have an idea! You can tell some of your funny stories. How about that story about the crazy kitty? Want to practice that now? That's such a great story."

"No."

I sighed. Peter looked over at me and raised his eyebrows.

"She'll be fine," I said. "As soon as she's around the other kids, she'll be her sweet, agreeable self."

I glanced into the backseat. Ruby was grimly picking

her nose and wiping it on the armrest of her car seat. When she saw me looking at her, she covered her eyes with her hands.

THE Heart's Song School was widely considered the best preschool in the city of Los Angeles. The competition for the seventeen spots that opened each fall in the Billy Goat room was cutthroat. It was probably easier to qualify for the Olympic gymnastics team. It was certainly easier to get into medical school. Everyone who was anyone in Hollywood had a little Billy Goat. The school's spring fund-raiser, a talent show, had boasted original songs by Alan Menken, dance numbers by Bette Midler, and one legendary reenactment of Romeo and Juliet's balcony scene starring Arnold Schwarzenegger and Whoopi Goldberg.

Our interview at the preschool took place with two other families. We perched on miniature chairs, covertly sizing each other up while waiting for the school principal. One family seemed pleasant enough. The parents were exhibiting the same slightly manic, good cheer as Peter and I. The father had a kind of artistic look, with longish, tousled hair. I decided he was probably a cinematographer or a moderately successful film director. He wore the same dress-up uniform as Peter, chinos and a slightly wrinkled oxford shirt. The mother was an attractive, dark-haired woman about my age, thirty-two or -three, wearing a long sweater over leggings and pretty brown boots. When she caught me looking at her, I smiled ruefully and rolled my eyes. She smiled back. Their son sat quietly in his father's lap and buried his head in his father's shirt whenever anyone looked at him.

The other couple was a whole different kettle of fish.

First of all, he was wearing a suit, a double-breasted sharkskin. Definitely Italian. He was substantially older than the rest of us, at least forty-five or fifty, but trying real hard to look thirty-five. He sported an expression that managed to look tense and bored at the same time. Skinny wasn't the word to describe his trophy wife. Emaciated more like. Her very young, twiglike body was wrapped in an elaborate slinky skirt with a Lycra top that revealed a strip of bare midriff. She sported a diamond the size of a small puppy on one finger. She had a gash of bloodred lipstick in an otherwise alabaster-white face, and her petulant pout precisely matched that of her daughter. I discreetly snuck a tongue out over my lips to see if I had remembered to put makeup on. Of course not. I rummaged in my purse for a lipstick, but had to satisfy myself with a tube of Little Mermaid Junior Lip Gloss.

The hyperelegant couple's daughter wore black velvet leggings and a red tunic with shiny black cuffs and pockets. Ruby was transfixed by her red patent-leather boots. She pointed at them and said, "Mama, buy me that"— *dat*—"I want *that!*"

Normally that kind of demand would be greeted with a minilecture on why we can't have everything we see. It is a mark of how desperately I wanted Ruby to get into that school that I leaned over and whispered in her ear, "I'll tell you what, kiddo. If you are really, really good I'll try to find you a pair of those boots."

The principal walked in just in time to hear Ruby say to the proud owner of the boots, "I'm getting those boots if I'm weawy good!"

I blushed to the brown roots of my red hair, and Peter snorted with laughter. The nice couple smiled and the not-so-nice couple looked superior. Trophy wife hissed "Morgan, come here," and hustled her daughter away from Ruby as if she imagined that my baby would try to wrench the boots clean off her little treasure's feet. As if Ruby would ever have tried that. At least not with me right there.

Abigail Hathaway, the founder and principal of the Heart's Song School, was a woman in her mid- to late fifties, tall, thin, and striking. She had black hair, shot lightly with gray, that she wore rolled in a chignon at the nape of her neck. Her clothes were gorgeous, conservatively elegant, and obviously expensive. She wore a faun-colored wool jacket buttoned loosely over a thick, creamy, silk blouse. Her skirt was in a matching herring-bone. It occurred to me to wonder how she kept herself looking so splendid when she was surrounded every day by forty or so frenetic and filthy preschoolers. Ruby and I had already managed to acquire matching milk stains on our shirts, and my shoulder was festooned with a pink splash of toothpaste where she had wiped her mouth after brushing her teeth. I looked like the "before" picture in a Calgon bubble bath ad. Abigail Hathaway looked like she was heading out to lunch at the hunt club.

She perched herself on the edge of a minichair, introduced herself, and told us how she had come to start this most elite and special preschool fifteen years before. I put on my alert and interested expression, the one I had perfected in law school to impress professors with my zeal and engagement with the material. Actually, I was listening with only about fifteen percent of my brain. The other eighty-five was concentrating on Ruby as she wandered around the room, picking up toys and books.

"Heart's Song is designed to be a place where children learn the most important of lessons, how to cooperate and communicate," Ms. Hathaway said. "To that end we try to inculcate values such as empathy and concern for others."

At that moment Ruby plucked a toy from the nice couple's son's hand. He began to cry.

"Look, Mama, I'm gwabbing!" she announced proudly.

"Ruby!" I snapped. "Don't grab."

"But Mama, I *love* to gwab." She smiled hugely. I shot a quick glance at Ms. Hathaway to see if she'd heard. She had and was looking at me expectantly.

"Ruby, these toys belong to all the children and we have to share." I was using my best Miss Sally, Romper Room voice.

"It's virtually impossible for children of this age to share, Ms. Wyeth," the principal said.

"Actually, it's Applebaum, Ruby and Peter are Wyeth, I'm Applebaum," I said automatically, then winced. Like I really had to make that particular point at that particular moment. I looked over at my daughter. "Never mind, Ruby."

At that point Peter decided to take over for me, since I was obviously not wowing the room with my parenting skills.

"Hey, Rubes, come over to Daddy." She ran over and jumped up into his lap.

The school principal continued on for a while, describing how at the end of the afternoon those of us who had been selected to move on to the next stage of the application process would be given forms to fill out and send in, along with the $125-dollar, nonrefundable application fee. After about five minutes of sitting quietly, Ruby had had it. She wriggled out of Peter's arms and leaped off his lap. She was making a beeline for the sand table and had mischief on her mind. As she blew by me, I reached out an arm, stopping her in midrun. I hauled her onto my lap.

"If we're all ready to settle down," said Ms. Hathaway

with a disapproving glance in my direction, "I'd like to tell you about the pedagogical goals of the Billy Goat program."

RUBY, it turned out, was on her best behavior after all. She played nicely and managed not to break anything. But none of that mattered. My parenting skills had not impressed Ms. Hathaway. As we gathered our belongings at the end of the morning, I watched as she handed a thick manila envelope to the pleasant couple, who, laughing delightedly, scooped up their shy little boy and rushed out the door. No packet came our way. I had a moment of sadness thinking that we probably would never get to know that nice family, who had seemed like people we could be friends with. Those thoughts were interrupted by a scene unfolding at the other end of the room.

"Excuse me. We haven't received our application packet." Morgan's father had reached his arm out to stop Ms. Hathaway as she walked toward the door.

"I'm sorry, Mr. LeCrone," she said.

"Sorry? What do you mean, you're sorry? Where is my application packet?" He leaned over her, threateningly.

"We are only able to extend an invitation to apply to a small number of those who visit. I am sorry."

"Look, what the hell are you talking about? Do you realize that I employ the parents of half your students? I suggest that you get me an application."

His wife put her hand on his arm. "C'mon, Bruce. Let's just go. Who gives a shit."

Ruby, who had been staring at the drama unfolding in the doorway, gasped. "She said 'shit,' Mama!"

I leaned down and picked her up. "Shh, honey-pie," I murmured. I wanted out of that room right away, but they were blocking the only exit. Peter and I looked at each other. Neither of us could figure out what to do.

"I give a shit, goddamn it. Who the hell do you think you are, lady?" LeCrone's grip tightened on Ms. Hathaway's arm. Two spots of color appeared high on her cheeks. She looked genuinely frightened.

"Bruce, I'm leaving right now," LeCrone's wife said, grabbing their daughter by the hand. She pushed by him, out the door. He opened his mouth to speak, but before he could say anything more, Peter walked over.

"Hey, let's just chill out here a minute. We're all a little tense. Nobody means any harm," my husband said as he put an arm around LeCrone's shoulder. "I don't know about you, man, but my back's killing me from those little chairs, and I'm seriously coffee-deprived."

LeCrone looked, for a moment, like he was going to snarl. But suddenly he seemed to change his mind. Angrily shrugging off Peter's arm, he spun on his heel and marched out the door. Ms. Hathaway sighed with relief. She hugged her waist with her arms and shivered.

"Mr. Wyeth, if you'll wait a moment, I'll go get you an application."

"That's okay. You don't have to reward me. We understand you have your selection process. It's no big deal," Peter said, motioning to me. I scooped Ruby up in my arms and accompanied him out the door.

"Thanks for everything and have a nice day," I said, smiling over my shoulder at the principal. I'm not sure what prompted that, maybe I just wanted to show her that we were fine and unscathed by her rejection. At any rate, it turned out to be a singularly inappropriate comment, given what happened later that evening.

Two

RUBY fell asleep in the car on the way home and Peter and I sat quietly, each immersed in private thought. I figured he was probably thinking about his latest script, the third in a lurid series about a marauding group of urban cannibals. It was definitely Peter's biggest movie so far, and he was under a lot of pressure to make the script satisfy all the various parties, including a director who spoke virtually no English and a studio executive with artistic pretensions.

When Peter and I had met in New York City, seven years before, he was working at Movie Madness, a cult video store in the East Village, and writing horror screenplays in his spare time. Actually, he'd been writing screenplays at work instead of waiting on customers. Our first conversation involved my threatening to report him to his boss and his asking me out for a beer instead. I still have no idea why I went out with him. It probably had a lot to do with his soft, sexy, gray eyes.

At the time Peter and I met, I had been earning the big bucks at a prestigious New York law firm. I married him six months after that first beer, fully expecting to support him for the rest of our lives together. Three weeks after we came home from our honeymoon (beach-hopping and rain-forest-trekking in Costa Rica), he got a call from his agent. Slasher movies were suddenly in vogue, and one of that year's hottest producers had gotten his hands on Peter's script for *Flesh-Eaters I*. He optioned it for more money than I made in a year.

Much to my joy, Peter's success allowed me to quit my job. The short and only answer to the question of why I had ever become a corporate lawyer in the first place was money. I graduated from Harvard Law School owing seventy-five thousand dollars. Delacroix, Swanson, & Gerard offered me a starting salary of just under ninety thousand dollars a year. After two years at the firm I had lowered my debt to a mere fifty thousand dollars, higher than my parents' mortgage but a slightly more manageable monthly payment than when I had started out.

During those two years I had billed six thousand hours, represented an asbestos manufacturer and a toxic-waste dumper, and helped to bust a union. My garment-workers'-union-organizing grandfather must have been spinning in his grave. I'd spent three weeks trapped in a warehouse in Jersey City, sifting through documents, and a month in a conference room in the Detroit Airport Hilton, listening to lying corporate executives. I'd done so many all-nighters that for a while Peter was certain I was cheating on him. The lunches at Lutèce and the Lincoln Town cars that drove me home each night were no compensation for the misery I felt during every one of my fourteen-hour days. By the time Peter got his big break, I was way past ready to quit.

We used Peter's advance to pay off my law school loans, packed the contents of our apartment into a U-Haul, hooked it to the back of my aunt Irene's 1977 Buick, and took off for the promised land, Los Angeles. We ended up in a 1930s apartment chock-full of period details and period appliances in Hancock Park, near Melrose Avenue, and I got the job I'd always wanted, as a federal public defender. For the next couple of years Peter wrote script after script, some of which were actually made into movies. We met a lot of interesting and creative people: writers, directors, and even an occasional actor. I represented gangbangers and drug dealers and became familiar with a side of L.A. that most of our new Hollywood friends tried to pretend didn't exist. I was the only one of our set not either writing a script, producing a movie, or trying to do one or the other. Nonetheless, I managed to hold my own at industry cocktail parties, regaling studio executives with stories about my cross-dressing bank-robber clients and how I was "protected" by the Thirty-seventh Avenue Crips.

I loved my job, and I was really good at it. Everything was going wonderfully, and we were really happy. And then something happened that destroyed it all: We had a baby.

Anyone who tells you that having a child doesn't completely and irrevocably ruin your life is lying. As soon as that damp little bundle of poop and neediness lands in your life, it's all over. Everything changes. Your relationship is destroyed. Your looks are shot. Your productivity is devastated. And you get stupid. Dense. Thick. Pregnancy and lactation make you dumb. That's a proven, scientific fact.

I went back to work when Ruby was four months old, and I quit ten months later. I just couldn't stand being apart from her and Peter. I'd call in the afternoon, snatching a few minutes to pump breast milk between court appearances and visiting clients at the detention center. Peter would tell me the latest cute Ruby story. I missed her first word ("boom") and the day she started to walk. Peter wrote at night, slept in, and took over for the nanny at eleven each morning. He and Ruby spent the day together, going to the park, playing blocks, lunching with pals from Mommy and Me. I was jealous. Completely, insanely jealous.

I was also doing a lousy job at work. I didn't want to be there any longer than I absolutely had to. I was relieved when clients pled guilty because that meant I wouldn't have to put in the late nights a trial demands. I finally realized that I was giving everything short shrift—my work, my husband, and most of all, Ruby.

So I quit. I dumped three years of Harvard Law School into the toilet and became a full-time mom. That decision blew everyone away, including me. My boss, the kind of working mother who came back to work when her kids were three months old and never looked back, thought I'd lost my mind. My mother kept me on the phone one night for two hours, crying. I was supposed to have the career she'd never been able to achieve. She felt like I had betrayed her feminist dream. My friends who hadn't yet had kids looked at me with a kind of puzzled condescension, obviously wondering what had become of the ambition that used to consume me.

As for myself, I couldn't really believe what I had done. For months, when people asked me what I did, I continued to reply, "public defender." If pressed, I would clarify by saying that I was on leave to be with my daughter. I never really came to grips with my status as a "stay-at-home mom." I'd always had just a little bit of disdain for women who devoted themselves completely to their families. I'd always assumed that they were home because they couldn't cut it, out in the real world. It had never occurred to me that a person would voluntarily leave a career in which she excelled in order to spend her days changing diapers and playing "This Little Piggy."

But that's what I had done. The worst part of it was that I wasn't especially proud of my skills as a mother. Ruby was turning out fine, if willful, stubborn, brilliant, and funny qualify as fine, but I wasn't any June Cleaver. I did all the things mothers aren't supposed to do. I yelled. I was sarcastic. I let her watch TV. I fed her candy and almost always forgot to wash the pesticides off the fruit. I never kept up with the laundry. My shortcomings as a mother bothered me enough to make me consider going back to work, but then I found myself pregnant again. That settled it. Awash in ambivalence, alternately bored and entranced, full of both joy and despair, I joined the ranks of stay-at-home moms. At least for the time being.

By the time we arrived back home from our debacle at the preschool, we were all sufficiently recovered from our ordeal to joke about it. Peter treated us to a dead-on imitation of Bruce LeCrone. Ruby and I invented a new game that consisted of pinching each other, shrieking "I love to gwab!," and then collapsing on the floor with giggles. By that evening our family's failure to enter the social register of the preschool set was forgotten.

After we had bundled Ruby into bed, and Peter had read that night's installment of *Ozma of Oz,* we settled down for the night. Peter went to work in his office, a converted maid's room at the back of our apartment, and I got into bed with my evening snack of ice cream and salted almonds. The calcium needs of my pregnant body provided sufficient rationalization for my astronomical ice cream intake. A few almonds made my decadent snack a protein-rich necessity. Or at least that's what I liked to tell myself. The increasing spread of my thighs I attributed to my body's stockpiling fat in order to breast-feed.

I flicked on the TV and spent the next couple of hours watching a movie about a woman with lymphoma whose anorexic daughter is sexually abused by a cross-dressing drug addict while a mudslide threatens their home (or something like that; I don't really remember). I was in hysterical tears from start to finish. I love watching disease-of-the-week films when I'm pregnant. That extra burst of hormones makes for a delightful two-hour sobfest. After the movie was over, I was about to turn off the set when the lead-in for the eleven-o'clock local news caught my attention.

"A prominent nursery school principal died tonight in an apparent hit-and-run. Angie Fong is live at the scene of the crash."

No way. It wasn't Abigail Hathaway. It couldn't be. After all, there were umpteen preschools and nursery schools in the Greater Los Angeles area. I stayed glued to the set through the commercial break.

The perky, helmet-haired news reporter stood in front of a cordoned-off street corner. Behind her I could see a mailbox tipped over on its side and crushed. I could swear I saw a woman's shoe lying next to it on the side-walk. As soon as I heard Abigail Hathaway's name, I yelled for Peter. He came rushing in to the bedroom, looking panicked.

"What? Are you okay? Is it the baby?"

I pointed wordlessly at the television.

"Abigail Hathaway, the founder and director of the exclusive Heart's Song School, was killed in an apparent hit-and-run outside of the school entrance this evening.

Witnesses say a late-model European sedan, either gray or black, swerved onto the sidewalk, crushed the victim against a mailbox, and then took off at a high rate of speed. No suspect has been apprehended."

The news reporter turned to a man in a baseball jacket with long, stringy hair. He was standing next to a shopping cart piled high with empty cans and bottles.

"Sir, you saw the accident?"

"It was no accident, man," he said. "This car comes speeding 'round the corner, goes up on the curb, bashes into her, and then takes off. I swear it was aiming right for her."

"And did you see the driver, sir?"

"Nah, but I saw the car. Silver Mercedes or maybe a black Beemer. Something like that. It was aiming for her, swear to God."

The screen switched back to the news anchor in the newsroom.

"Police are asking that anyone with any information about this incident please call the number on the bottom of your screen."

A commercial began, and I switched off the set. I had this strange, nauseated feeling in the pit of my stomach.

"Oh, my God. I just can't believe it. We saw her today. *Today.*" I felt tears rising up in my eyes. Peter sat down on the bed and pulled me to his chest. I started to cry.

"I know, honey, I know," he murmured, stroking my hair with his hand.

"I don't know why I'm crying," I said, sobbing. "I didn't even like her."

"I know, honey."

I stopped my tears. I had the hiccups. "I'm okay. Really. You can go back to work."

"You sure?"

"Yeah, it's okay. I'm going to call Stacy." Stacy was an old friend from college, whose six-year-old son was a graduate of Heart's Song. Peter went back to his office and I dialed the phone.

"Hello?" Stacy's voice sounded groggy.

"It's me. Sorry to wake you, but have you heard?"

"What?"

"Somebody killed Abigail Hathaway."

"What?" She perked up. "Are you serious? What happened?"

"I was just lying here watching the news. We didn't get in, by the way. And they come on with this story about how somebody mowed her down with their car. I couldn't believe it. I started crying."

"What do you mean, you didn't get in? She didn't give you an application?"

"No. Anyway, are you listening to me? The woman is *dead*!"

"Jeez. Wow. It was a car accident?"

"Yes. I mean, no. She was on the street outside of the school and some car hit her and then took off."

"Outside of the *school*?" Stacy sounded horrified. "Outside of Heart's Song?"

"Right on the corner. A car hit her and knocked her into a mailbox. At least I think that's what happened. Anyway, she's dead."

We talked for a while longer, speculating that the driver must have been drunk. I told Stacy about the interview and described the scene between the angry father and Ms. Hathaway.

Suddenly something occurred to me. "Oh, my God, Stace. Maybe he killed her! Maybe he freaked after not getting into the school! Maybe he snapped!"

"Oh, for Pete's sake, Juliet. He did not kill her. Bruce

LeCrone is a studio executive. He's the president of Parnassus Studios. And he used to work at ICA. He's not a murderer."

Stacy is an agent at International Creative Artists, one of the most prestigious talent agencies in town. She knows everybody in Hollywood.

"How do you know what he's capable of?" I said. "You didn't see this guy. He was furious. Insanely furious."

"Juliet, Bruce LeCrone's temper is legendary. That was just par for the course with him. You should hear how he treats his assistants."

"I still think there was something bizarre about how angry he got. I think I'm going to call the cops and let them know what happened."

"I really don't think that's such a hot idea. If you make trouble for LeCrone, and he finds out it was you, Peter will never sell a script to Parnassus. You don't want to go throwing wrenches into your husband's career just because you have some wacked-out theory."

That stopped me in my tracks. I certainly didn't want to ruin Peter's chances of doing a movie with one of the biggest studios in town.

"I'll talk to Peter about it before I do anything."

"You do that."

"So, what were you up to tonight?" I asked.

"Nothing! What do you mean? What are you suggesting?"

"Jeez, Stacy. Get a grip. I wasn't suggesting anything. I just wanted to know what you were up to."

"Oh. Nothing. I worked late."

"Poor you."

"Yeah, poor me."

We said good night and I turned off the light. Shivering, I snuggled down into my bed, tucked my body pillow under my heavy belly, and pulled the down comforter up to my chin. I couldn't seem to get warm. It was a long while before I fell asleep.

ABIGAIL Hathaway's homicide happened too late at night to make that morning's *Los Angeles Times,* but the morning news shows each aired the story. I watched all three networks and got three very different stories. One referred to the death as a traffic accident. Another said the police had suspects under investigation. The third reported that the police were treating the death as a hit-and-run and were looking for the driver, whom they believed might have been under the influence of drugs or alcohol. Much to my embarrassment, I found myself vaguely disappointed that it appeared to have been a random accident. Over the course of my long, sleepless night I had worked up a head of steam about Bruce LeCrone. He seemed decidedly murderous to me.

The problem with having experience as a criminal defense lawyer is that you tend to see criminal violence everywhere, in everyone. One of Peter's and my biggest sources of conflict is that despite the fact that he spends his days thinking up new and exciting ways for people to be killed, preferably with as much blood and pain as possible, he is an eternal optimist who always believes every human being to be basically good at heart. I've spent too much time with apparently normal guys (and some women, too) who've done heinous things and am always willing to believe someone capable of extreme violence.

Not surprisingly, we got into an argument when I told Peter that I was suspicious of LeCrone. I had just woken him and was standing in the doorway of my closet, desperately searching for something to wear. Ruby was happily ensconced in the living room, glued to *The Lion King*.

"Oh, right, Juliet," Peter said, obviously irritated. "That's what most studio heads worth nine bazillion dollars go around doing. Murdering preschool teachers."

"He's not most studio heads! Tell me you didn't think he was psychotic."

"I didn't. Aggressive, yes. Used to getting his own way? Yes. But psychotic? No. If he's psychotic then so are two-thirds of the executives in Hollywood."

I thought about that for a moment while I rummaged through a pile of trousers, looking for some maternity leggings. Stacy had said the same thing, and it did have a ring of truth to it. Peter was always regaling me with stories of his dealings with various producers. One guy, in particular, was legendary. He had a phone with buttons on it marked "rice cakes"; "diet Coke"; "sushi." If he punched a button and his assistant didn't show up immediately with the requisite item, heads rolled. This same producer was famous for having been arrested on a flight from New York to Los Angeles for refusing to give up the in-flight phone and screaming obscenities at the flight attendant who tried to pry it away from him. He was probably single-handedly responsible for the appearance of phones on the backs of airplane seats. Bruce LeCrone was certainly no more horrifying a character than he.

On the other hand, as far as I knew, neither the flight attendant nor any of the assistants of the ranting and raving producer had ended up dead. It was one of LeCrone's enemies who had gotten herself mashed against a mailbox by a luxury car.

However, giving my already stressed-out husband

grounds for an anxiety attack was not on my list of appropriate activities for the day. I decided to drop it—or at least to let Peter think I had.

"You're right. I know you're right. Listen, you remember I'm supposed to be having lunch with Marla?" Marla Goldfarb was the Federal Public Defender, and my old boss.

"Was that today?"

"Yeah. I told you yesterday. Is that a problem? Do you have a meeting this afternoon? Can you watch Ruby?"

"Sure, no problem. I was going to take her on a comic-book-store crawl, anyway." Peter's idea of a good time is hitting every comic-book store in Hollywood in a single afternoon. If he doesn't get the latest *Hellboy* or *Eightball* on the very day it's issued, he's completely inconsolable.

"Thanks, sweetie." I finally found a pair of leggings with relatively intact seams, threw one of Peter's freshly laundered dress shirts over it, and accented the ensemble with a jauntily tied scarf. I looked at myself critically in the full-length mirror. At least my hair looked good. I'd dyed it to match Ruby's red curls. I'd even kept dying it while pregnant, figuring that the damage to the baby from an ugly and depressed mother would be worse than whatever the hair dye might do to him.

"Not bad for a fat girl," I said.

"You are NOT fat. You're pregnant. You look great." Peter walked over to me and slid his arms around my waist, his hands gently cupping my protruding belly. I leaned back against his chest and smiled. My husband always knows how to make me feel sexy. The night before I gave birth to Ruby, he gave me a black, lace maternity negligee and told me that nothing turned him on like the sight of my huge, pregnant body. What a guy. I have no idea if he was telling the truth, but I decided to believe him. We're both convinced that the subsequent events were what put me into labor. Who needs labor-inducing medication when you've got a willing and able man around?

Three

THE office of the Federal Public Defender is in downtown L.A., in the U.S. Courthouse. I had always loved
appearing in those courtrooms; the large, wood-paneled
rooms have a solemn ambience that well matches the
seriousness of the proceedings that take place there. The
defender offices are, on the contrary, fairly typical,
hideous, government offices with dingy carpeting and
glaring, fluorescent lights. The low-rent atmosphere
never helped convince my clients that their lawyer was
competent and capable. Criminal defendants, like the rest
of the world, tend to believe the old adage "You get what
you pay for." Since the indigent don't have to pay their
appointed counsel, they usually feel like they are getting
their money's worth. The constant battle to convince drug
dealers and bank robbers that I was good enough for
them had contributed to the malaise that eventually pre-
cipitated my departure from the office.

Walking into the office that day, I felt an almost overwhelming pang of nostalgia and longing. I missed the place. I missed going to court. I missed my clients. I even missed the lunatics I used to work with. Criminal defense lawyers are a strange lot, arrogant and usually somewhat nuts, but genuinely and fiercely committed both to their clients and their ideals. You need a special personality to take on the forces of the government day after day, particularly when most people despise what you do and generally feel quite comfortable telling you that. I can't count how many times people have asked me, usually in tones bordering on disgust, what I would have done if I ever found out that a client of mine was guilty. I always reply that the real question is what I would have done if I had ever found out that a client of mine was innocent. The truth is that I probably would have collapsed with horror. If you do your best, lose, and a guilty person goes to jail, at least you can sleep at night knowing you've done your job. If you do your best, lose, and an innocent person goes to jail, that could pretty much ruin your life. Since, no matter how good a lawyer she is, most of a public defender's clients end up in jail, defending a truly innocent person would be a nightmare.

I tamped down my emotions enough to have a nice lunch with Marla. I even managed to limit my discussion of Abigail Hathaway's death to my feelings of shock and my ambivalence over whether to tell Ruby. I refrained from accusing prominent local businessmen of murder. When we got back from our Chinese chicken salads, I said good-bye and went out to the elevator bank, punched the down button, and tried to resist the little voice in my head. If the elevator that showed up hadn't been bulging with blue-suited prosecutors, I might have gone home that day, and avoided all the stress and fear of the next few weeks. But, as luck would have it, there was no room for a pregnant woman and no suit feeling chivalrous enough to give me his spot. The door closed and instead of hitting the down button again, I walked back into the federal defender's office and headed to the lair of the investigators. I've never been very good either at resisting temptation or minding my own business. That's what made me such a good lawyer.

No criminal defense lawyer could function without the assistance of an able investigator. These are often retired cops who see nothing strange in their decision to spend their golden years keeping people out of prison after having spent their youth putting people in. My favorite investigator was a man named Al Hockey, an ex-LAPD detective who took a bullet to the gut in his twenty-fifth year on the force. Al had tried to play golf for a year or so after leaving his job, but at a mere fifty was too young to spend his days chasing a little white ball around a green lawn. He'd been with the federal defender's office going on ten years, and during my time as an attorney there we were a terrific team. The first time we'd worked together, he'd managed to drum up fifteen bikers, each of whom claimed to have slept in my client's camper and most of whom surprised the heck out of the prosecutor, judge, and jury by acknowledging more than a passing acquaintance with methamphetamine. It didn't take the jury long to decide that any one of them could have left the packet of crank in my client's glove compartment. That was my first not-guilty verdict.

I walked into Al's office, plopped myself into a beat-up vinyl armchair, and put my feet up on the desk.

"Hey, old man. Miss me?"

Al knocked my feet to the floor and flashed me a huge grin.

"I was wondering if you were going to grace me with your presence. I heard you were around today."

"Wow, you must be using your keen detective skills again, Al."

"You know it, fat girl."

"I am not fat," I sputtered. "I'm pregnant."

"Whatever. All I know is that it's been a mighty long time since I've seen you in your leathers."

I'd earned the eternal devotion of the sexists in the investigator's office by showing up on my third day of work in a black leather miniskirt coupled with a conservative black blazer. I liked to pretend that I was making a statement, but the truth was I had spilled coffee that morning on the skirt that matched the blazer and, since I had eaten French fries and pie at every truck stop between New York and California, my mother's old leather mini (circa 1960) was the only thing in my closet that fit. I've never regretted my fashion *faux pas*. It can be next to impossible for an aggressive woman to earn the respect and cooperation of her colleagues, particularly if those colleagues are a bunch of beer-bellied, bellicose ex-cops. For some reason, my willingness to seem decidedly female, even sexy, made the guys feel better about accepting me as an equal. I wasn't someone they had to watch themselves around for fear of being reported for sexual harassment. Perversely, wearing a leather miniskirt made me one of the guys.

"Peter's keeping you barefoot and pregnant, Juliet." Al laughed.

I lifted a sneaker-shod foot. "Well, pregnant anyway," I said.

"What exactly is it that you do all day?"

"Oh, you know, bake cookies. Drive car pool. Run the PTA."

He looked at me seriously. "And that's enough for you?"

I had no ready answer. No, it wasn't enough.

"It's enough for now." I said and then changed the subject. "So Al, I have a favor to ask."

"A favor?" Al asked, his eyebrows raised.

"Yeah. Nothing big. Well, not too big. Well, maybe kind of big. Will you run someone through NCIC for me?"

NCIC stands for National Crime Information Center. It's the computer system listing everyone with a criminal record in the United States. The investigators have access to it so they can get the skinny on the informants, witnesses, and other nefarious characters the defender's office deals with. They are specifically not allowed to use it to, for example, check if someone's daughter's fiancé has a record. Al's daughter was, by the way, still single despite a couple of offers.

Al got up, poked his head out of his office door, looked up and down the hall, and sat back in his chair.

"Got a name and Social for me?"

"No Social Security number, but I do have the name. Bruce LeCrone."

"Capital 'C'?"

"Yeah."

"What about a birth date?"

"No, but he's probably about forty-five or fifty years old."

"Okay, give me a minute." Al scribbled the name on a Post-it and headed off down the hall to the computer terminal with the NCIC link. While he was gone I nosed around the files on his desk. Nothing seemed very interesting, just the usual bank robberies, mortgage frauds, and drug deals. Ten minutes passed before Al came back.

"Well, your boyfriend's got a record."

"No kidding! Great. Fabulous. He's not my boyfriend. Gimme that." I grabbed the printout.

In 1994 Bruce LeCrone had pled guilty to chapter 9, section 273.5.

"Do you know what section 273.5 is?" I asked Al.

He looked over my shoulder. "No idea. Here, look it up." He handed me the blue, paperback *California Penal Code*.

I leafed through the book, found the appropriate section, and read aloud, "Willful infliction of corporal injury. Any person who willfully inflicts upon his or her spouse—"

"Domestic violence," Al interrupted.

"A batterer." I said.

I was flabbergasted. I knew how prevalent domestic violence is, even in educated, wealthy families. Nonetheless, it still shocked me to hear that someone in my world was a wife-beater. Recent events notwithstanding, most of us probably still believe that that kind of thing happens only in trailer parks, not in Brentwood.

"Any jail sentence?" Al asked.

I looked back at the printout. "Nope. Probation."

Al leaned back in his chair and looked at me speculatively. "Juliet, what gives? What are you up to?"

"What do you mean?" I asked, disingenuously.

"You know what I mean. Are you working on something?"

I considered whether to take him into my confidence. I trusted Al, I always had.

"I'm checking into the background of a man I think might be responsible for a murder. Have you been paying attention to the case of the nursery school director who was hit by a car?"

"I think I saw something about it on the local news. What's your connection to the case?"

"I knew the woman."

"So you're playing detective?"

"I'm just looking into a few things."

"That sounds like so much nonsense to me."

"What?" I was genuinely shocked.

"Look, Juliet, the cops can do their job. They don't need you investigating this murder, if that's even what it is. They'll figure out who done it without any help from you."

I sputtered.

"This is about *you*," he continued. "You are doing this for yourself."

I shrugged, angry at him but knowing, deep down, that he was right.

"You've always been a ball of fire, Juliet. It was obvious from that first day I saw you come in here looking like Tina Turner. You just like mixing it up."

"That's probably true," I admitted.

"Not much opportunity for that, driving around in that big blue Volvo of yours, is there?"

"Nope. There isn't. What do you want me to say, Al? That I'm playing private eye because I'm bored with the daily grind of motherhood?"

"Well, are you?" He asked.

I considered for a minute. "Probably. Is there anything wrong with that?"

Al looked at me and shrugged. "How should I know? Who do I look like, Dr. Laura?"

I had to spend a few minutes promising Al that I wasn't involved in anything dangerous before I could gather my things and leave.

I drove home, strangely excited and energized by my discovery. I walked in the door to find Ruby and Peter immersed in an art project that involved sprinkling purple glitter all over the kitchen floor. I was about to berate the two of them for their sloppiness when Ruby held up a piece of paper covered in glitter and crayon.

"Look, Mama. This says 'I love you, Mama, because you are so beautiful.' " My eyes filled with tears as Peter and I smiled hugely at each other over Ruby's head. Sometimes it just takes you by surprise. Who was this fabulous little person careening around our house, and exactly what had we done to deserve her? How could I possibly consider leaving this delightful creature and going back to work?

Four

THAT evening Peter, Ruby, and I went to dinner at one of our regular restaurants, Giovanni's Trattoria. Giovanni himself greeted us, as usual, and scooped Ruby up in his arms, taking her back to the kitchen to be petted and spoiled by his brother, the chef, and his mother, a sweet old woman in a long, black dress whose sole job seemed to be criticizing her sons and feeding bits of canoli to my daughter. Peter and I sat down at our usual table in the corner near the kitchen, and ordered a bottle of mineral water. Giovanni had known I was pregnant before my own mother did. He figured it out the night we declined our usual bottle of pinot noir and asked for one of fancy, Italian sparkling water instead.

"I'm getting the pasta with clam sauce," Peter said.

"That's what I want. Get something else."

"You know, Juliet, we can both order the same thing. It won't kill us."

"God forbid. That's the difference between you WASPs

and the rest of us. Two people dining together cannot order the same thing. What's the point of sharing if we both order the same thing?"

"What if I don't *want* to share?"

"Then you should have married Muffy Fitzpatrick from the tennis club instead of Juliet Applebaum from the delicatessen." I smiled sweetly at my husband and reached out to take the piece of bread he had put on his plate, just to illustrate my point. "You get the clams. I'll get the Arabbiata. And we share."

Peter smiled and grabbed his bread back.

"So, Juliet, what are we going to do about preschool?"

In my investigative zeal I had completely forgotten about what had involved me with the whole Hathaway affair to begin with.

"Oh, God. I don't know. We didn't even get an interview at Circle of Children or First Presbyterian. Maybe we could just forget about it. Do kids *have* to go to preschool? Wait, I have a terrific idea! We'll home-school her!"

"Right. I can definitely see you doing that. I can see you preparing elaborate lesson plans with multicolored charts and stickers while you're cooking up a batch of homemade papier-mâché and creating dioramas of early Colonial life. And all this with a baby attached to your breast. That is just so *you*, Juliet."

I shot my husband a glare. "Okay, maybe I'm not the most patient parent in the world, and maybe I've never done finger painting or played with Play-Doh or made a model of the Eiffel Tower out of Popsicle sticks, but don't you think I could handle it for a year?"

He looked at me balefully.

"How was your lunch with Marla?" he asked, changing the subject.

"It was fine. The office is hiring again."

Peter raised his eyebrows.

"No, no. I'm not thinking of going back. I'm seven months pregnant. How could I go back?"

"But you want to." Peter was trying to look as if he didn't care whether I went to work or not. Yet I knew how much he liked having me home. It wasn't a sexist impulse, but rather a selfish one. He liked the companionship. He liked the idea of being able to rush off spontaneously to Paris or Hawaii or Uttar Pradesh even though, in reality, we never rushed off anywhere more exciting than Home Depot.

"No," I answered quickly. "Not really. I mean, I wouldn't mind having something to do for a few hours a week, but I'm definitely not interested in full-time work!"

"Oh, good. I was afraid you were getting bored."

"Just because I'm bored sometimes and just because I'm not some kind of arts and crafts supermom doesn't mean I want to leave you guys. I love staying home. Really. I love it." Maybe I could convince myself if I said it often enough.

Peter looked relieved. I decided to take advantage of the goodwill I had engendered.

"I found out something interesting about our friend Bruce LeCrone."

"Juliet." His mood was not as receptive as I had thought. "I thought we decided you were going to give that a rest."

"*We* didn't decide anything. You did. And, anyway, I'm not doing anything. I just checked to see if he has a record."

"That seems like doing something to me." Peter looked irritated.

I said nothing. I could see his curiosity slowly getting the better of him.

"Does he?"

"Excuse me?" I asked mock-innocently.

"LeCrone. Does he have a record?"

"Oh, so you *are* interested."

"Fine, don't tell me." He frowned and began earnestly studying the menu.

"He was convicted of domestic battery."

"Domestic battery?"

"You know, wife-beating."

"Holy cow!" Peter exclaimed.

"Exactly what I said. I was on the right track after all."

Peter looked doubtful. "Just because he beats his wife doesn't mean he killed Abigail Hathaway."

"Maybe not, but it sure does mean he's capable of violence. Anyway, I think it must have been his ex-wife. The charge is seven years old, and unless he married the present Mrs. LeCrone when she was in junior high, I don't think she's the one he beat up. Although, I suppose he could be beating her, too. Did you notice any bruises on her?"

"Don't get carried away, Juliet. Granted, this doesn't make him look good, but it's hardly evidence of murder." Peter poured some olive oil onto his bread plate, dipped his bread, and took a bite. "Still, I guess we should tell the police about his fight with Hathaway."

"You read my mind, my love." I reached out with my napkin and wiped away the trail of oil dripping down his chin.

At that moment Ruby came running out of the kitchen, chocolate smeared all over her chin.

"Giuseppe made me fed-up-cino alfwedo. Is that okay?"

"Sure, Peanut," Peter said. "But only if I get a bite."

"No, Daddy. Alfwedo is only for me an' Mama today. Right, Mama?"

"Right, kiddo," I said, somewhat amazed that Ruby was sharing with me rather than her dad. When faced with a choice between the two of us she never picked me.

Peter turned back to me. "Do you want me to call the cops for you?"

"Of course not. I'm the one who figured this out; I'm the one who should call. And I'd like to ask them one or two questions about the investigation."

Peter smiled. "Be sure to tell them you were a public defender. That'll put them right in your corner."

THE next day I called the Santa Monica Police Department and asked to speak to the detective in charge of the Hathaway investigation. I was connected to the homicide unit and spoke to a woman who informed me that Detective Mitch Carswell was out of the office but would return later in the day. I told her that I had information regarding the death of Abigail Hathaway, and she said she would pass my message along to Detective Carswell. He called back later that afternoon while Ruby and I were making Play-Doh pasta.

"Juliet Applebaum?"

"This is she. Ruby, not in your mouth!"

"Detective Carswell, Santa Monica Police Department. I understand you called regarding the Hathaway case?"

"Yes, I did. Ruby! Can you hold on for a second, Detective?"

Without waiting for his answer I quickly put the receiver down on the table, leaned across, and hooked my finger into Ruby's mouth. Over her screams of protest I scooped out clumps of turquoise blue Play-Doh.

"But it's *pasta*!!" she shrieked indignantly.

"For heaven's sake, Ruby. It's pretend. It's pretend pasta. You can't eat it!"

PlaySkool puts huge quantities of salt into its Play-Doh with the idea that that will make it unpalatable and prevent tiny sculptors from consuming their medium. This precaution is wasted on a child whose idea of a snack is sucking the salt off of an entire bag of pretzels.

I picked up the receiver again.

"Sorry. I have a two-year-old and I'm trying to keep her from killing herself."

Detective Carswell didn't laugh.

"I'm kidding," I said, just to make sure he didn't actually show up at my door with an arrest warrant and a couple of social workers from the Department of Youth and Family Services.

The silence on the line was deafening.

"Are you still there?"

"Yes, Mrs. Applebaum. Can you talk now, or shall I call back at another time?"

"Ms. And now's fine."

"You have some information for me regarding the Hathaway hit-and-run?"

"Yes. That is, I think so. I mean, I have the information, but it may or may not be relevant to the Hathaway case."

"Why don't you let me be the judge of that," Detective Carswell said.

"Right. Sure. Um, where do I begin? My husband, daughter, and I were at Heart's Song, that's the school Ms. Hathaway ran."

"I'm familiar with it."

"Of course you are." Did I detect a note of sarcasm? "We were there for an admissions interview with two other couples. At the end of the morning, one of the people there got into a fight with Ms. Hathaway."

"A fight?" Carswell interrupted. "What kind of fight?"

"It was actually pretty ugly. Ruby! Stop that! Put that Play-Doh down, *now!*" I pried the purple gunk out of my daughter's hands and did my best to scrape it off the underside of the kitchen table.

"Detective, hold on a sec, okay?" I put the receiver down again.

"C'mon, honey, let's watch a video."

I loaded up *The Lion King,* a film that by a conservative estimate Ruby has seen 237 times, hit the play button, and picked up the receiver again.

"Sorry. Where was I?"

"There was an ugly fight at the preschool."

"Right. This one guy, Bruce LeCrone, grabbed Ms. Hathaway and started yelling at her because she didn't accept his daughter to the school."

"She told him that at the interview itself?"

"I know. Pretty obnoxious. They have this procedure where they give out applications to the families who move on to the next step of the application process. She gave one to this other couple but not to LeCrone or us."

"Wait a minute." Carswell sounded genuinely astonished. "You people were applying to *preschool,* right?"

"Well, yes, but this isn't just any preschool. It's a really good school and it's very competitive." As I explained this to the detective I became decidedly embarrassed at being involved in the whole preschool rat race. What were we thinking? If we ended up in this kind of frenzy over preschool, imagine the horrors of college applications!

"Let me get this straight. You all come for an interview, and at the end she only gives an application to the people she likes?"

"Right."

"And she didn't like you?"

"Right. I think she thought I was beating my kid."

"Excuse me?" He sounded confused and a bit suspicious. "You were beating your child?"

"No, no!" I nearly shouted. "It's just that Ruby was about to destroy the sand table and I grabbed her and . . . oh, never mind. It's not relevant. I don't know why I even mentioned it."

Detective Carswell sighed. "What exactly is the *relevant* information you have for me?"

I really needed to get to the point. I could almost hear his thought: "Who is this crazy broad who's wasting my time?"

"Bruce LeCrone's daughter didn't get in either. He began yelling at Ms. Hathaway and grabbed her arm. He left without doing anything more, but I think he's worth investigating. He has a criminal record for domestic violence!" I ended, dramatically.

Detective Carswell didn't respond.

"He beat his wife!" I continued just in case he hadn't understood.

"Mrs., er, Ms. Applebaum, how is it that you are familiar with his criminal record?"

Now it was my turn to be quiet.

"Are you a friend of his wife?" he asked.

"No. Nothing like that. Anyway, I think it was his ex-wife."

"How do you know about his record?" he repeated.

I paused. "I'd prefer not to answer that question. But, if

you don't believe me, feel free to check it out on your own. It's capital L, E, capital C, R-O-N-E."

"I'll do that," Detective Carswell said. "I have a few more questions for you, if you don't mind. For starters, why is it that you prefer not to answer my questions?"

"I have no problem answering your questions, just not that particular one." I knew I sounded defensive, but I couldn't help it. No way was I going to get Al into trouble.

I peeked into the family room, where Ruby was singing about how she couldn't wait to be king.

"Go ahead. Ask away," I said.

"Abigail Hathaway rejected your daughter from the Heart's Song School?"

"Right."

"And that upset you?"

"Of course. Wait a minute. Are you actually suggesting that I killed her?"

"I'm not suggesting anything. I'm just trying to get my facts straight."

"Fine. We were rejected at the school. We spent the rest of the day at home and I was in bed when I found out that Ms. Hathaway was killed. The phone rang any number of times during the evening, in case you want to verify my alibi."

"There's no need for that."

The detective paused. "Ms. Applebaum, now, I want to make sure you understand that the Santa Monica Police Department is doing everything we can to find the driver of the car that hit Abigail Hathaway. Leaving the scene of an accident is a very serious offense and, rest assured, we intend to find the person who did this."

"I'm glad to hear that."

"Ma'am, we deal with cases like this all the time. Drivers operating under the influence, uninsured drivers, they drive off after an accident all the time. But we'll find him. We usually do."

"So you're certain that this was a hit-and-run?" I asked. "Aren't you even considering the possibility of murder?"

"We haven't ruled out anything, ma'am."

"Good." I could hear myself starting to get a little snippy. That invariably happened when I was confronted with the hyperpolite condescension of your average police officer. I changed my tone. "Thank you for calling me back."

"That's quite all right, ma'am. Good-bye."

And he hung up.

I stared moodily at the receiver. I considered the idea that Detective Carswell might view me as a suspect in Abigail's murder, but pretty quickly dismissed that. Peter and I had each other as alibis and, if the detective was crazy enough to investigate a hugely pregnant woman, I could always pass a lie detector test. They might not be admissible in court, but they usually convince a prosecutor of a suspect's innocence or guilt.

What really worried me was that it sounded like the detective wasn't looking that hard for anyone to suspect of murder. In a city replete with drive-by shootings, gangland-style hits, and domestic murders, a simple hit-and-run car accident, even one that cost the life of a prominent citizen, wasn't going to get much police investigation. I'd seen it before. The cops would put a few signs up in the neighborhood, friends and family would raise funds for a reward, and in a year or two people would ask, "Hey, did they ever find out who ran over poor Abigail Hathaway?"

I sat down on the couch and pulled Ruby into my lap.

Idly twirling her curls in my fingers and humming "Hakuna Matata," I puzzled over my next step. Detective Carswell wasn't going to change his approach to this case just because some housewife told him to. The truth was, he was probably right. It probably wasn't a murder, but rather at worst a vehicular homicide—drunk or reckless driving. But Bruce LeCrone's past made him worth investigating. And if the cops weren't willing to do it, I could. After all, this was something I'd been trained to do, and something I was actually very good at.

Only a very small fraction of a criminal defense attorney's job involves dancing around a courtroom turning prosecution witnesses into quivering lumps of jelly. The vast majority of the job is investigation. The lawyer has to figure out what happened—not what the police say happened, and sometimes not what actually happened, but what, if any, scenario exists to make her client's claim of not guilty at least plausible. That involves long hours at crime scenes, interviewing witnesses, talking to family members, and more. If a client is convicted, there's even more investigation to be done. The lawyer has to find enough information to convince the judge that a lighter sentence is warranted. It's all about fieldwork, and I had always loved that part of the job. There was no reason I shouldn't exercise that atrophied muscle in the service of Abigail Hathaway. At worst, I'd find out nothing. And, maybe, just maybe, I'd discover something that would give the police a reason to consider the possibility of murder.

I was still puzzling out my next step an hour later, when Ruby danced over to the VCR and pressed the rewind button.

"Wanna play trains, Mama?" she asked.

I sighed, already bored at the prospect of toddler games. I looked at my watch. I had a whole hour to kill before I could expect to see Peter walk through the door and relieve me of my Romper Room duties.

"Why don't you play by yourself, Ruby."

I looked up in time to see a fat tear rolling down my baby's face.

"You never wanna play with me," she whispered.

"Sure I do. I play with you all the time. Don't I?"

"No."

I thought for a moment. She was right.

"Okay, honey, let's play trains," I said, pushing thoughts of Bruce LeCrone and untimely deaths out of my mind and lowering my substantial bulk onto the floor.

Ruby hauled out her plastic bin full of Brio trains and tracks. Peter had brought the little magnetic train set home with great fanfare as part of our campaign to ply Ruby with gender-neutral and boy's toys. She loved it from the moment she set eyes on it. Much to Peter's horror, however, she was not at all interested in setting up the tracks and making the little train run around them. Instead, she liked to play "train family." Lately, the train babies all had bad colds and were in bed, being cared for by the train mommies. The engine, in its role as train doctor, gave them frequent shots and pills. These games drove her normally patient father to distraction, and I'd once heard Peter wail, "Can't they just pull *a heavy load*?"

Balancing a little caboose on my round belly I said, "Hey look, Rubes, the train baby is stuck on top of a mountain! Can the train mama rescue her?"

By the time Peter got home we'd been playing for close to an hour and my eyes had long since glazed over.

What was it about me that made it so hard for me to enjoy these games? Peter loved playing with Ruby. I often saw other mothers playing with their kids. Was I the only one who found it cataclysmically boring?

At the sound of the garage door opening, Ruby and I rushed to the front door like a couple of golden retrievers who'd been left alone all day. Peter walked in wearing his gym clothes and carrying a brown paper bag that gave off the most tantalizing aroma.

"Guess what?" he said.

"What?" Ruby shouted.

"I went to the gym and guess what?"

"What?" she shrieked again.

"What's next door to the gym?" He matched her yell.

"What?" This time I thought the windows would shatter.

He lowered his voice to a stage whisper. "Barbecue!"

Peter and I had celebrated the pink line in the pregnancy test by ordering a pizza—stuffed, no less—and had been going strong ever since. While he didn't quite match me inch for inch, Peter's belly was slowly creeping outward. I found this to be a considerable comfort. The last thing a rotund, pregnant woman needs is a guy with a washboard stomach lying next to her in bed.

We feasted on our ribs, dipping the pieces of spongy white bread that Ruby liked to call "cottony bread" into the barbecue sauce. Finally, chins and fingers sticky and stomachs content, Peter hustled Ruby off to her bath and bed. I picked up the receiver. Stacy was where I knew she'd be at seven-thirty at night. At work.

"Hey."

"Hey to you, too. Did Bruce LeCrone confess yet?" she asked.

"Ha, ha, ha. You'll all be sorry you gave me such a

rough time when the guy's trying to run the studio from San Quentin."

"Oh, please, Juliet. You are really being ridiculous. Seriously, have you found out anything new?"

I brought her up to date on my phone conversation with the police detective and what I had found out about LeCrone. When I told her about the domestic violence charge she gasped.

"Oh, for crying out loud, Juliet, you are so full of it," she said.

"What are you talking about?" Sometimes Stacy really made me angry. "I am not full of it. I put his name through the computer. The guy was convicted of beating up his wife."

Stacy was silent.

"Stacy? Are you still there?"

No reply.

"Stacy, come on. Would I lie to you?"

She sighed. "No, I suppose not."

"Look, I need some information from you," I continued.

"What?" She sounded suspicious.

"Nothing too big. I just need to know LeCrone's address."

"Oh, for God's sake, Juliet. I'm not going to give you his address."

"Why not?"

"Because he used to be a colleague. He worked here before he left to run Parnassus. I can't just give you a colleague's address."

"Well, can you tell me approximately where he lives?"

"No!"

"Just look it up on your database. Don't give me the address, just the neighborhood. C'mon, I'd do it for you," I wheedled.

She fell silent for a moment and then said, "Are you sure about this domestic violence thing?"

"Absolutely. I couldn't be more sure. I saw the printout of his record myself."

"All right. Give me a second, I'll check in the computer." She sounded grim. I heard her tapping a few keys.

"He lives in Beverly Hills a little east of the Century City Mall."

"Near Roxbury Park?"

"I think so," Stacy said.

"That's a nice park," I said. "Ruby would like it. Maybe we'd better go check it out."

"I'm not even going to bother telling you to be careful, Juliet. It doesn't do any good."

"I'm careful. I'm just taking my daughter to the park. What could possibly be wrong with that?"

Five

THE next morning dawned warm and beautiful. It was one of those days that remind you that Los Angeles is just a desert covered in freeways and parking lots. The light was so bright it hurt my eyes, but it seemed as likely to be emanating from the white lines in the road as from the sky above. I usually greeted this kind of day with a scowl and a muttered, "Great, another beautiful day. Who needs it?"

Not so today. Today we had plans. Ruby and I donned matching purple sunglasses and, careful not to wake Peter, gathered up her pails and shovels and headed out to Roxbury Park, a lovely expanse of green grass, play structures, and *bocci* and basketball courts on the southern end of Beverly Hills. The children playing there generally reflected the demographics of the neighborhood, primarily wealthy white kids with a smattering of Iranians and Israelis who'd made good in the jewelry, film, or air-conditioning business.

When Ruby and I arrived we found the play area packed with toddlers. I dumped Ruby's sand toys out in the pit and set her up next to a dark-haired little boy with a bulldozer, and a little girl with blond pigtails who was making sand pies. Ruby and the tiny chef immediately struck up a conversation and I headed out to the benches, satisfied that she was busy for a while at least.

As in all Los Angeles area parks (and maybe those in all affluent cities), the benches were strictly segregated. About half were populated by a rainbow coalition of women—Asians, Latinas, black women with lilting Caribbean accents. Those women chatted animatedly, sharing bags of chips and exotic-looking treats, stopping only to scoop up fallen children or take turns pushing swings. The children they watched over were, without exception, white.

The tenants of the other benches were the Los Angeles equivalent of the suburban matron, of whom there are two distinct types. One group, with impeccably mani-cured nails and carefully blow-dried hair, called out warnings to their little Jordans, Madisons, and Alexan-dras. The other group, the ones I liked to think of as "grunge mamas," were just as carefully turned out, in contrived rags artfully torn at knee and elbow. They wore Doc Martens and flannel shirts, and their shouts of "Watch out for the swing!" were directed at little boys named Dallas and Skye and little girls named Arabella Moon. I belonged somewhere between the two. My over-alls disqualified me from membership in the Junior League, but, since I'm a lawyer and not a performance artist or jewelry designer I wasn't quite cool enough for the alternative music set.

It took me only a moment to spot Morgan LeCrone.

She sat on the top of a high slide, looking imperiously down at the children playing below her. Behind her, a towheaded boy whined for his turn down the slide. At the bottom, a middle-aged Asian woman waved both hands wildly, beseeching the child to go.

"Morgan, time come down. Come down, Morgan. Other children want play, too."

Morgan ignored the woman.

I walked over and stood next to the Asian woman, who obviously had the unpleasant job of nanny to the LeCrones' spoiled princess.

"Mine does that. Drives me nuts," I said, smiling.

"She never come down. She go up and sit. I always gotta go up and get her."

"Maybe if you just leave her she'll have no choice but to slide down on her own," I suggested.

"You think that okay?" the woman asked.

"Sure. I think that would be fine. Let's just walk over to that bench and have a seat. She'll come down."

I led the woman over to a nearby bench under a shady tree and she sat down, clearly happy to get out of the glaring sun.

"My name is Juliet," I said, holding out my hand.

She took it. "I'm Miriam, but everyone call me Lola."

"That means grandmother," I said.

"You know Tagalog?" she said, surprised.

"Not really. My daughter, Ruby, has a friend who's Filipina, and she calls her grandmother Lola."

"Yeah. Lola mean grandmother. All my kids calls me Lola."

"Do you baby-sit for other kids or just Morgan?"

"She my only one now but she number thirteen for me. I got six of my own, too." Lola looked proud.

Reminded of her charge, we both looked up in time to see Morgan fly down the slide, hair blowing out behind her, a huge smile on her face.

"Hmph. That something I don't see alla' time," Lola said. "She don't like to smile."

"No?" I asked. "That must be pretty hard to deal with."

"I tell you something: I take care lotta kids in my life. I got six my own kids, I been nanny plenty times. But this kid the hardest. I call her Amazona, she always hittin' and beatin' other kids. She even hit me!" Lola shook her head, obviously scandalized at Morgan's misbehavior.

I murmured sympathetically, shaking my head.

"It's okay. I love her anyway. I love alla' my kids." Lola leaned back against the bench. "Which one yours?"

I pointed to Ruby, who was still busy in the sand pit.

"Nice red hair. She get it from you," Lola said.

I smiled. "I hope not! I get it from a bottle."

"You lucky! Everybody think yours real because of her."

I pulled a pack of gum out of my pocket and handed her a piece. We sat, companionably chewing, for a moment.

"So, do you like being a nanny?" I asked.

"I love my kids," Lola repeated.

"And the job?"

"That depend. Some jobs I like more than others."

"I guess it must depend on the family."

"Yeah, mostly it the family. If the kids happy. If the mom and dad happy. One time I work for couple in the middle of divorce. That was terrible. Poor kids."

"Are Morgan's parents good to work for?" I asked nonchalantly.

Lola paused. "They okay. Not so bad. They not there so much, so it's okay.

"Her parents both work?" I asked.

"He workin' alla' time. She, I dunno, maybe she shoppin' alla' time."

"They don't spend much time with Morgan?"

"No. The father sometimes go work inna morning before she awake, come back after she asleep. Don' see her all week. They go out every night. Never even eat dinner with that kid!"

"That's terrible! You wonder why some people have children. What's the point if they're not going to spend any time with them?"

Lola and I nodded, agreeing with each other. I glanced over at Ruby, who had come upon Morgan playing on the slide.

"I know you!" I heard my daughter shout. "Mommy! I remember her!"

Hurriedly, I tried to distract Lola. The last thing I wanted was for her to discover that I had ever seen Morgan before. "So, do you live in?" I asked.

"Yeah. First Monday to Friday, but now they pay me extra and I stay all weekend, too."

"You work seven days a week?"

"Sure. They pay me fourteen dollars a hour. My daughter in medical school in Manila. It's very expensive."

"I'll bet. When's the last time you had a day off?"

"Not so long ago. Monday night she tell me go home. She gonna stay in."

My ears pricked up. This was just the information I was looking for!

"Wow. They both actually stayed home with their daughter for once," I said, with just the slightest hint of a query in my tone.

"Her, but not him. I put Morgan to bed, I clean up, I go to my sister's house. I left maybe eight-thirty. He not home yet."

Pay dirt. Abigail Hathaway was run down on Monday at about nine in the evening. Bruce LeCrone may have had another alibi, but he wasn't home immediately before the murder.

I decided to try to find out if LeCrone's violent tendencies had reared their ugly head.

"You know, Lola, I just read this article that said that men who work all the time are more likely to be violent. You know, like hit their wives or their kids." Embarrassingly unsubtle, but what the heck.

Lola got very quiet.

"I wonder if he's like that. Like what the article said." I pressed.

She said nothing.

I pushed harder. "Do you think he might be like that?"

"He don' hit that baby, I know that. I would never let him hit that girl," Lola blurted out. She was clearly hiding something but just as clearly worried about how much she had already said.

"I gotta go. It late now," she said, gathering her bag.

"Wait!" I said. I hadn't gotten nearly enough information from her. I decided to bargain that Lola's antipathy toward her employers would keep her from giving me away. Reaching into Ruby's diaper bag, I rustled around until I found an old business card. Crossing out the federal public defender's phone number, I scrawled in my home number. "Please give me a call if anything happens, or if you want to talk, or anything," I said, pressing my card into her hand.

Lola nodded quickly, crammed my card into her pocket, jumped up, and rushed off to the slide, where Morgan had once again begun her slow, deliberate assent. She scooped the little girl off the ladder and, despite Morgan's howls of protest, hustled her off the playground.

"See you again!" I called after her retreating back.

"Okay. Bye," Lola said, without stopping or even turning back to look at me.

I'd obviously touched a raw nerve. I believed the nanny when she said that LeCrone didn't hurt Morgan. Not because I didn't think him capable of beating his child, but rather because I didn't think Lola would stand for it. That little Filipina grandmother seemed perfectly capable of protecting her charge. Her reaction, however, made me think that LeCrone's capacity for violence was not unfamiliar to the members of his household. It seemed pretty likely that he was beating up on someone, and I was willing to bet that it was his wife.

While all this was certainly disturbing, it didn't get me any closer to proving that the man had killed Abigail Hathaway. All I'd succeeded in doing was ruling out one possible alibi.

I decided to put the LeCrones out of my mind for the time being and went over to Ruby, who was wistfully watching the children on the swings.

"Hey, big girl! You want me to push you?"

"Yes! As high as the sky, Mama! As high as the sun, moon, and stars!"

"Hey, what a coincidence! That's how much I love my girl! As much as the sun, moon, and stars," I said, kissing the top of her head. I picked her up and deposited her on the swing.

"I got a coincident, too, Mama. Mines is that I love you as much as there are elephants in the zoo!" Ruby squealed, her legs kicking in the air as the swing rose higher and higher.

"That's a lot of elephants, Sweetpea." I pushed her again. For one of the few times in my life I was distracted completely from everything except my daughter, rushing toward the glare of the sunless sky, her copper curls shining and her mouth open in a yowl of glee. My breath caught as I tried to freeze that moment in my memory. I wanted to be sure I never forgot her that way, full of joy and absolutely certain that the world is a wonderful place, a place where Mama is always there to push, it's possible to reach the moon on a swing, and the zoos are bursting with elephants.

six

THAT night Peter and I had planned one of our infrequent, much-anticipated date nights. I fed Ruby her favorite dinner, macaroni and cheese. I tossed in a couple of microwaved broccoli florets (which would, of course, never actually pass Ruby's lips), and I had a well-rounded meal sure to satisfy even the most scrupulous of nutrition advocates. Okay, not the *most* scrupulous, but good enough for me.

Once Ruby had finished her macaroni and cheese and pushed her broccoli into a pile at the side of her plate, I rousted Peter from his office, where he was pretending to work but really busily clicking his mouse and slaying Ganon and other cybervillains.

Once I'd convinced him that it was really time to go, I yet again found myself standing naked in my room, idly scratching my itchy belly and studying the contents of my closets, like I expected to find lurking therein a Sasquatch, a paving stone from the lost city of Atlantis,

or the propeller of Amelia Earhart's airplane. Or, at the
very least, something to wear. Early in my first pregnancy
I had excitedly gone to a maternity store, happily imagining myself in all sorts of elegant ensembles that artfully
disguised my girth while showing off my glow. Yeah,
right. Elegant is not what the designers of maternity wear
have decided is the appropriate look for their corpulent
clientele. "Cute" is the adjective of choice. Bows, rib-
bons, little arrows pointing down at the belly. Prints of
smiley faces and happy flowers. Lots of pink.

I don't know who decided that pregnancy requires the
infantilization of a woman's wardrobe, but I'd like whoever
it was to spend a few moments with me while I model those
outfits. It's hard enough for me to look like a grown-up,
since I'm only five feet tall. With my width fast approach-
ing the same dimensions as my height and my face assum-
ing the proportions of the moon, the last thing I needed was
a frill on the collar of a pastel blue ruffled smock.

I'd stocked my closet with black leggings and oversized shirts in neutral colors. Each day I resolutely tried
to find a new and interesting combination. Raiding
Peter's wardrobe helped alleviate the monotony, but that
was becoming less of an option as I slowly but surely
inched up toward and, horrifyingly, past his weight. I was
outgrowing his clothes as fast as I had outgrown my own.

Tonight I was determined to look decent. Peter and I
were going to a movie premiere. We didn't often get
invited to these Hollywood events. We're not exactly A-
list material. However, the producer who'd optioned
Peter's latest script had just released a new film, a typical
shoot-'em-up action movie starring a taciturn, kickboxing Swede who made Steven Seagal look like a candidate
for the Royal Shakespeare Company. While the movie
was bound to be both jarringly loud and earth-shakingly

dull, I was looking forward to the premiere hoopla. It had been quite some time since I'd hobnobbed with Hollywood's elite.

I dragged on a pair of my ubiquitous black leggings, hauled them up over my belly, and confronted my closet yet again. A flash of sequins caught my eye. There, in the back of my closet, lurked a seemingly ill-advised purchase, a sequined shirt of clingy spandex in a deep, shining green. I'd bought it years ago when I went through a brief club-hopping phase. I used to wear it tucked into that leather skirt. I pulled the shirt over my head and snapped it down over my bulging belly.

There are, I believe, two ways to dress when pregnant. One possible avenue hides the belly under loose, smock-like tunics. It is the more obvious choice. The second celebrates the size of the belly, calling attention to its contents. Green sequins drawn tight enough to see the outlines of my navel fall squarely into the latter category. It was a risk, but I have to say it worked.

I made up my eyes elaborately and chose a dark red lipstick. I jammed my puffy feet into open-toed platform sandals and waddled into the bathroom.

"So? Whaddya think?" I asked in my best Jewish-princess-from-Long Island voice.

Ruby was sitting in the tub, her hair full of shampoo and pulled into triceratops horns at the top of her head. Peter sat on the floor next to her, attacking her with a three-inch, blue *T. Rex* figurine. They turned to look at me.

"Wow, Mama, you look so fancy!" Ruby said, smiling.

"Wow, Mama, you look so sexy!" Peter said, leering.

My two loves, each with trashier taste than the other.

"Do I look good enough for Hollywood?"

"You look good enough to eat," Peter said, grabbing a fistful of my rear end and squeezing.

*   *   *

ANDREA, Ruby's anorexic baby-sitter, showed up on time for once. As usual she had brought a Tupperware container full of carrot sticks and celery stalks. I'd long ago gotten over asking her to help herself to the food in our kitchen. For a while I'd even provided her with her favorite veggies, but to no avail. She always brought and ate her own. It was as if she thought our carrots had soaked up extra calories by virtue of their presence in our fat-polluted fridge. Like the bacon was secretly rubbing itself on them when the door was closed.

Eating disorders aside, Andrea was a great sitter, responsible and creative. Ruby loved her. They were playing a round of Candyland as we left, and Ruby didn't even look up to say good-bye.

Peter parked the car as close as he could to the movie theater, but it was almost a ten-minute walk before we arrived at the edges of the bleachers that had been set up for the Swede's adoring fans. By that time I was limping in my platform shoes and holding my stomach with both hands, hoisting the load off my bladder. Peter gripped me by the elbow, propelling me through the throngs of hysterical kickboxing fanatics, many of whom actually seemed to be practicing their favorite moves while they waited for their idol to appear.

"Hey, watch it, pregnant woman here!" he said, deflecting a Nike that grazed my belly.

We finally made it to the police barricades set up to keep the crowds off the red carpet leading into the theater. Peter thrust his engraved invitation into the face of one of the security guys manning the entrance. The guard motioned us through a gap between two barricades, and we stepped up on the red carpet. The area in front of the theater was lit by a huge phalanx of hot, white Klieg lights. The carpet was crowded with reporters fawning over stars and thrusting microphones in their faces. As we stepped up, the crowd of hoi polloi behind the barricades turned in one motion to look at us. An audible sigh of disappointment escaped them as they realized we were nobody. A camera operater who had turned his oversized video camera in our direction snapped off the light and turned away, leaving us in a little, dark island of anonymity in the midst of the bright, star-filled field of red. Peter and I looked at each other and smiled ruefully. There's nothing like a Hollywood opening to make you feel like you don't exist.

We walked quickly up the carpet toward the door of the theater. Suddenly, a hand reached out and grabbed my arm, jerking me roughly. I staggered, my balance thrown off. Peter threw his arm around my waist to keep me from falling, and I turned around to see where the hand had come from. I found myself staring up at the beet-red face of none other than Bruce LeCrone. He was already screaming by the time I turned my head.

"Who do you think you are, you bitch! I'm going to have you arrested for stalking! What the hell do you think you're doing? Do you know who I am, you disgusting cow?"

My mouth dropped open and I stared at him blankly, utterly taken aback by his invective. Not even my creepiest clients had ever abused me that way.

Before I could gather myself together to blast him back, Peter took hold of LeCrone's hand, wrenching it off my shoulder and pushing it away.

"Back off. Back off, now," Peter said quietly.

LeCrone leaned into Peter's face. "Your wife has been following my nanny around, accusing me of beating up my kid. I'll kill her *and* you!"

Peter, his white face and set chin the only outward evidence of how truly angry he was, put his hand on LeCrone's chest and pushed him gently but firmly away.

"No one has accused you of anything. Now we're going to turn around and go into the theater and I suggest you do the same."

By now everyone was staring at us. The reporters had stopped in midinterview. The videographer who had previously considered us too boring to merit his attention had his camera trained firmly in our direction. From the corner of my eye I could see two security officers rushing our way.

"Look, I happened to bump into your nanny at the park and we got to talking, that's all," I said, hoping to calm the furious man down. What had possessed Lola suddenly to turn loyal? Peter turned to look at me in surprise.

"You just happened to ask her if I beat up my kid? Bullshit!" LeCrone said, his voice only slightly quieter than a shriek.

"Can we just cut out the screaming?" Peter said. "There's obviously been some kind of misunderstanding here."

"Exactly," I interjected. I decided to go for broke. After all, I couldn't get the guy any *more* furious than he already was. "I was actually trying to find out if you had an alibi for the night Abigail Hathaway was killed."

LeCrone exploded. With a bellow, he reached his arm back and shot out a fist, aiming it directly at my face. Peter jumped in to deflect the blow, managing to put his shoulder between LeCrone's balled hand and my nose. Peter took the punch and staggered back with the force.

LeCrone was getting ready to deliver another strike when the two security officers finally arrived at our sides. They grabbed LeCrone, one on each arm, and hauled him back a few feet. One raised a warning hand at Peter.

"That's it, buddy," the officer said.

As they hustled LeCrone off, he turned back and shouted over his shoulder, "I was at a reception at ICA, you dumb broad. That's my *alibi*." The last word was delivered in a snide snarl.

I turned to Peter, who was staring at me, shaking his head.

"I guess he has an alibi," I said sheepishly.

At that moment a long white limo pulled up at the curb and the Swede leaped out the door, arms outstretched to greet his public. A roar rose up from the crowd, and all attention was diverted from us and toward the evening's kickboxing prince.

"Juliet, what in God's name were you thinking? Are you trying to get yourself killed?" Peter said as he grabbed my hand and dragged me into the theater.

"Hardly," I responded. "I just asked his nanny a question. How was I supposed to know that the guy would lose his mind?"

We walked down the aisle and found ourselves two seats toward the back.

"Might I remind you that you yourself called him psychotic and capable of murder?" Peter said.

I settled myself into the chair. "Yeah, well, I guess I didn't realize exactly how psychotic. Anyway, he has an alibi." I reached across Peter's body and gingerly touched his hurt shoulder. "I'm so sorry, honey. Are you okay? Does it hurt?"

"Yes, it hurts. And don't touch me," Peter said, wincing and shrugging my hand off his shoulder.

"My knight in shining armor. My hero," I said, smiling sweetly.

Peter snorted and turned his face to the screen. I could tell that under his irritation was a wellspring of macho pride happily bubbling to the surface. He'd protected his woman!

"Thank God you were there. I swear he would have knocked me out if you hadn't deflected that punch," I said, leaning my head against his good shoulder and staring up at him admiringly.

Peter grudgingly reached his arm around me and gave me a squeeze.

"I love you," I said.

"I love you, too. Even if you are an idiot." He smiled despite himself. "I was about to really let him have it when those security guards showed up."

"It's lucky you didn't. You're in much better shape than he is and you probably really would have hurt him," I said, exaggerating more than a little but not more than necessary. A man's ego is a fragile thing. It never hurts to give it a few pats every once in a while.

We settled in to watch the movie.

News travels fast in Hollywood. Bad news faster than good, and misinformation at the speed of light. By the time we got home that night our answering machine was blinking like a hopped-up cokehead with a twitch. Peter's agent had called to ask if he had given any thought to his career before punching out the head of Parnassus Studios. My prenatal Yoga teacher had called because she'd heard I'd been beaten up and gone into early labor. Stacy left a hysterical shriek on the machine, shouting, "Juliet, my God, are you okay? I heard that you got into a fistfight with Bruce LeCrone at the premiere of *Rumble in Ran-*

goon! Did he hurt you? My assistant just told me that LeCrone knocked Peter out and had to be dragged off by four cops! What did you say to him? Are you nuts, Juliet? Are you totally insane? Call me as soon as you get this message. Call me right now!"

I called.

"Hi, Stace. It's me. I'm fine. Nothing happened."

"What do you mean 'nothing happened'? Everyone is talking about this. The only people not talking about this are lying under slabs at Forest Lawn. What in God's name happened?"

"Nothing happened. Nothing serious. LeCrone started screaming at me at the theater in front of every camera in Los Angeles, and that's about it. Except that he also tried to punch me but Peter got between us. Peter's fine. LeCrone hit him on the shoulder."

"And no one's in the hospital?"

"No, unless they locked LeCrone up in the booby hatch, which I hope they did because that is clearly where he belongs."

"But what did you *do*? Why did he try to kill you?"

"Oh, for crying out loud, he did *not* try to kill me. Jeez, Stace, you're beginning to exaggerate worse than I do! He took one tiny punch."

"But what did you *do,* Juliet? People don't just hit other people for no reason, not even studio executives."

"Nothing, really. I just met his nanny in the park. I might have asked her if she thought he might have any violent tendencies. Nothing more than that." I sounded defensive, but I knew she would flip out. And she did.

"Are you kidding me? What are you *doing*? What did you *expect* to happen? My God!"

"Well, it's all moot now, and anyway, I'd like to point

out that you could have prevented this whole incident if you'd told me that LeCrone was at one of *your* parties on Monday night."

"What? One of *my* parties?"

"He said he has an alibi. He said he was at an ICA cocktail party."

"Monday night? Monday night. What was Monday night?" She seemed to be flipping through a mental calendar. "Oh, right! Monday night was the unveiling. We had a cocktail party to celebrate the new Noguchi piece in the office lobby. I think I even remember seeing him there, now that you mention it."

"Gotta say, Stace, I wish you'd remembered this a couple of days ago," I said, trying not to sound irritated. After all, it wasn't Stacy's fault that I was playing Hercule Poirot.

"Gotta say, Jule, it never occurred to me that you would be accosting LeCrone's household employees in the park. Otherwise, I might had worked harder to provide him with an alibi."

Stacy wouldn't let me hang up until I'd promised to leave the sleuthing to the professionals with the badges and the guns. I crossed my fingers and vowed to concern myself with more appropriate things, like whether I'd have another C-section or manage to deliver the new baby in the old-fashioned way or where we would send Ruby to preschool now that Heart's Song was no longer an option.

As I returned the handset to its cradle it suddenly occurred to me that perhaps Abigail Hathaway had been killed before putting her official rejection in Ruby's file. Maybe we should apply again! I wouldn't want to present too obvious a motive to Detective Carswell, but, on the other hand, I had Ruby's future academic career to think about.

Peter came in from walking Andrea to her car and locked the front door behind him.

"Sorry your agent is so mad at you," I said.

"Don't worry about it. You know, I think that's the first time *she's* called *me* in about two years!" He kissed me on the forehead and headed off to the bathroom to get ready for bed.

I followed him and we brushed our teeth side by side, alternating spitting in the sink. I pulled off my sequin shirt and leggings and climbed into bed. I dragged the full-length body pillow up alongside me and tucked one end up under my belly. As I was plumping the other pillows into position, Peter lay down on his side of the bed.

"Construction complete yet?" he asked.

"Almost," I said, giving the pillow behind my back a last punch and settling down with a groan.

"You're going to have to redo the whole thing in ten minutes when you get up to pee."

"I know. Isn't being pregnant fun?"

He put his head down on the lone pillow I'd grudgingly left for his use. Looking up at the ceiling, he said, "Well, at least this whole thing is over. We know LeCrone didn't murder Abigail Hathaway, and you can stop obsessing over this."

"I suppose," I said.

Peter sat up. "Juliet!"

"What?"

"Your own best friend gave him an alibi. What more do you need?"

"I suppose," I said again.

Peter rolled his eyes.

"Look," I said, "doesn't it just seem a little pat to you? I mean, why would Stacy suddenly remember that she'd seen him? I talked to her the night of the murder. I even told her that I suspected him. So why didn't she tell me then? Why didn't she give him that foolproof alibi then?"

That seemed to bring Peter up short. He paused for a moment and then shook his head. "You know what, Juliet? I don't care. All I care about is that next time, you might just get one of us killed. Promise me that you're not going to do any more investigating."

"You're right. Of course you're right. I'm sorry I even mentioned it." I didn't promise anything.

"Are you working tonight?" I asked.

"Yeah," Peter said, and hoisted himself up off the bed. "See you in the morning."

"I love you."

"Me, too. Good night."

Seven

THE next morning I woke Peter up at eleven o'clock, as usual.

"I have a midwife's appointment today," I said as I handed him his coffee.

"Thanks." He took a sip. "Do you want me to come?" When I was pregnant with Ruby, Peter had come to every single prenatal appointment. This time around he missed them more often then not.

"No, that's okay. It's just a standard eight-month checkup. And I might go to prenatal Yoga afterward."

"Okay. Ruby and I'll go to the Santa Monica pier, maybe ride the carousel."

I gave him a kiss. "See you later," I said. I had the afternoon to myself.

Dorothy, my midwife, shared offices with an acupuncturist and a massage therapist. The place had seemed a little kooky to me at first, but I had gotten used to it. Stacy had convinced me to use Dorothy instead of an obstetrician and, just as she'd promised, my prenatal care definitely had a more personal touch this time around. I'd gotten pretty sick of my old doctor asking me if I had any questions with her hand on the doorknob and her body half out in the hall, heading to the next patient.

When I got to the office, I took off my shoes and stepped onto the scale. Gasping in horror, I stripped off my socks. No substantial difference. I took off my glasses, headband, and earrings. The scale began to wiggle a bit, like it was considering whether to cut me some slack. It decided not to. I'd gained seven pounds in the previous four weeks. I was tipping the scales at a cool 170. If the NFL was in the market for any short, female linebackers, I was ready to answer the call.

I was tempted to take off my shirt, leggings, bra, and even my panties to try to bring the numbers down out of the leviathan and into the human range, but the scale was in the hall, and there were a couple of expectant fathers milling about. Modesty prevailed.

Once inside the exam room, I listened patiently to Dorothy's lecture about the dangers of excessive weight gain, and lay on my back as she palpated my belly.

"Little guy been kicking much?" she asked.

"Less than before," I said. "That's normal, right?"

"Sure. There's less room for him to move around in there. He's getting big!"

I smiled, imagining a big, fat boy curled up inside of me.

"How are you doing, Juliet? You seem much happier to me. Last month you were a little blue." Sometimes Dorothy seemed almost psychic. She immediately sized up my state of mind, and even seemed to know better than I how I was doing. She considered the emotional health of her patients to be as important to a successful pregnancy and birth as their physical condition. My emotions had been on something of a roller-coaster ride over the past eight months.

I considered what she had just said. "You know, I *am* happier." I hadn't even noticed. "I've actually been feeling pretty good for the past few days!"

"Terrific. Is something going on? Are you involved in a new project?" she asked.

"No, there's nothing going on. Not really. Maybe I'm just getting used to the idea of having another baby. It's about time."

"True, true," she said. "I've been hoping this would happen for a while now. Let's listen to the baby's heart."

I lay back as she moved the portable Doppler over my belly. After a few false starts we heard the rapid thump-thump of my baby's heartbeat. My eyes welled up for a moment as I imagined him, this mysterious new creature, so completely familiar to me and so totally unknown.

"He sounds great. And he's perfectly in position, with his head down," Dorothy said.

"Hi, baby Isaac," I murmured.

"So it's Isaac?" Dorothy asked.

"Yup. We let Ruby choose between Isaac and Sam. She actually wanted to name him Odysseus but we nixed that."

"Odysseus! My goodness."

"She knows her Romans," I said, smiling proudly.

"Greeks."

"Right. I knew that."

Dorothy bustled around the room, putting away her instruments. She reached an arm out for me to hoist myself up off the table. I got myself dressed, scheduled my next appointment for two weeks hence, and went out to my car. I squeezed myself behind the wheel and turned on the radio to my favorite talk-radio station. Unfortunately, the Fates were conspiring to keep me involved with Abigail Hathaway. I tuned in just in time for the hour's news wrap-up, including an announcement that crowds of Hollywood luminary-parents were expected at the preschool director's memorial service, to be held at two o'clock that afternoon. I looked at my dashboard clock. It was one forty-five.

For a split second I actually considered going to my prenatal Yoga class and forgetting about Abigail, LeCrone, and the whole Heart's Song debacle. For a split second, only. I made a U-turn on Santa Monica Boulevard.

Naturally, there was valet parking. I gave the keys to my Volvo station wagon to a perky young blonde in a blue jacket with "Valet Girls" embroidered on the pocket. She could barely contain her disgust at the state of my car, which really irritated me because I had thoughtfully swept the used Kleenex, dried-out baby wipes, partly eaten apples, ancient Ritz crackers, chewed-up plastic dinosaur, and slightly rancid sippy cup of milk off the passenger seat and onto the floor. Maybe she was just disappointed because she had to park a beat-up old station wagon instead of a brand-new Porshe. As Ruby would say, tough noogies.

I walked by the ubiquitous television cameras and into the chapel. The pews were crowded, and I saw a surprising number of children's faces. My impression of her skill with children to the contrary, Abigail Hathaway must have been popular with her students. I was scanning the rows, looking for a spot large enough for my considerable bulk, when I heard a voice.

"Juliet! Juliet!"

I looked over my shoulder and spotted Stacy seated near the back of the chapel. She was wearing a severe black suit that showed off her creamy, white skin. Her thick, blunt-cut, blond hair was hidden under a hat that was, perhaps, a bit too elegant for a funeral. She leaned down her row, and with a flash of red nails motioned to her pewmates to move over. Miraculously, a space was made. I squeezed in, apologizing to those I mashed on the way. I've never figured out what is the appropriate way for a pregnant woman to move down a row of seats. Do you stand with your belly toward the people you are passing, impaling their noses on your jutting navel? Or do you go rear end first, forcing them to contort away from that particular body part? Obviously both options are an exercise in tackiness, but which is worse? I opted for the butt-in-the-face on purely selfish grounds—I wouldn't have to look at them while I squeezed by—and sat down next to Stacy.

"How come you didn't tell me you were coming?" I whispered.

"It never occurred to me that you'd be here. I mean, you didn't get in, right?" Stacy didn't whisper. Up and down the row, heads swiveled in my direction. I blushed.

"Nice, Stace."

"Sorry."

"Forget it. What a turnout!" I said, changing the subject.

"I know! Unbelievable. Look over there. There are Nicole and Tom sitting next to Michelle. She's a client of ours. Michelle! Hi, Michelle." Stacy waved at the movie star, who stared back, nonplussed.

"For God's sake, Stacy, this is a funeral, not a cocktail party! Keep your voice down!" I said.

Chastened, Stacy assumed a stage whisper. "So, what are you going to do about preschool?"

"I don't know. We missed the deadline for most places."

"What were you thinking?" Stacy seemed genuinely disgusted. "How many schools did you apply to?"

"Three. And we got rejected everywhere."

"Three? That's it? Are you nuts?"

A woman in the row ahead of us turned around to get a good look at the mother of the preschool reject. I smiled at her and waved. She blushed and turned back around.

"Stacy, can we just drop this? I'll figure something out."

"No, we cannot drop this. This is terrible. You don't seem to understand. If Ruby doesn't go to the right preschool, there is no way she'll get into a decent elementary. Then you can kiss high school good-bye. And let's not discuss college. This is a crisis. An absolute crisis."

"You mean a crisis as in the AIDS crisis? The dissolution of the Soviet Empire? The massacres in Rwanda? Would you please get some goddamn perspective?" I was hissing like an angry rattler.

Stacy looked at me and rolled her eyes. "We'll talk about this later. Maybe there's someone I can call."

"Oh, my God, really? Is there? I'm sorry for losing my temper. Do you really think there's something you can do?" My own indignantly expressed sense of perspective lasted about fifteen seconds. Stacy patted my hand and turned back to scanning the crowd.

"You see down front? That's Abigail's husband, Daniel Mooney. He's a real estate developer or something." She pointed out a tall man in his mid- to late fifties, with salt-and-pepper hair done up in long, Byronesque curls falling to his shoulders.

"*That's* her husband?" I was astonished. "That hippie dude is married to her?"

"Was. And he's not a hippie. He's more of a Boho, Euro-trash type. Except I think he's from Iowa or something. Her daughter is sitting next to him."

Abigail Hathaway's daughter looked to be about fifteen. My heart went out to her as she sat there, a chubby adolescent with a pale face trying unsuccessfully not to cry. Her hair was dyed a sickly purple and shaved on one side. She had obviously tried to tone it down for her mother's memorial service, combing the long side over the top and clipping it with a plain, tortoiseshell barrette. There was a foot of space between her and Daniel Mooney. Neither so much as glanced at the other. He looked straight ahead, and she stared into her lap.

"Poor thing," I said. "Why doesn't her father put his arm around her or something?"

"Oh, that's not her father," Stacy replied. "He's Abigail's third or fourth husband. They'd only been married for a few years. Audrey's father was her first husband, I think. Maybe her second."

"Abigail Hathaway had four husbands? Are you serious?"

"Three or four. I don't remember."

Just then the hall filled with the sound of an organ, and we all hushed. A small man in a cleric's collar walked solemnly onto the altar, raised his hands to the gathered mourners, and led us in a hymn. Stacy pointed out the words in the hymnal, but I didn't need to look. I'd memorized Judy Collins's rendition of "Amazing Grace" long ago. I even knew the harmony.

I found most of the service remarkably moving, but then I've been known to cry at Lysol commercials. One of Abigail Hathaway's oldest friends gave the eulogy, recalling her as a wonderful wife, mother, and a resource to the entire community on child-rearing. A moderately famous movie star, the father of a student at Heart's Song, wiped away tears as he told us how Abigail Hathaway had helped his daughter through the difficult period of her parents' moderately notorious divorce.

After the movie star sat down, the pulpit remained empty for a few moments. Suddenly, with a toss of salt-and-pepper curls, Daniel Mooney rose from his seat. He stepped up to the pulpit with a long, loose stride and lifted his arms to the assembly.

"I embrace you. I embrace you and thank you for your love, for your support, for your memories of our dearest Abigail.

"I see that some of you are crying. Don't cry for her. Life is simply an illusion. The tears you shed are for yourselves, for us all. For we are here in the time-space of earthly life and she has gone forward, gone upward to the realm of complete being. She has gone home.

"If you grieve for Abigail you will hold her back from that place. You will hold her back from the light. Celebrate for her. Be joyful for her. Let your joy propel her ethereal body to the home we all crave."

Daniel Mooney blathered on in this manner for a good half hour and actually succeeded in drying up all the tears that might have been shed for his wife. Periodically during his oration, he would pause dramatically and sweep his hair off his forehead with a flourish of thumb and ring finger. And, he never, not once, looked down at his stepdaughter, sitting alone in the front pew, isolated and abandoned in her misery. By the time he finally sat down, I had found another suspect in Abigail Hathaway's death.

The minister led us in a final hymn, then stepped down off his pulpit and led the dead woman's husband and daughter out of the chapel. Once they had walked down the aisle, the rest of us stood up to leave. Stacy turned to me and said, "Do you want to grab something to eat? I don't have to be back at the office for an hour or so."

"Who, me? Eat? Never," I replied.

As we made our way through the crowd, Stacy stopped every few feet to greet another one of her acquaintants.

"Hello! Tragic, isn't it?" she said. And again.

"How *are* you? Isn't this just awful?" And yet again.

"Hi. So sad. Isn't it just so sad?"

I was impressed at her capacity to sound both genuinely grief-stricken and happy to see someone at the same time. We finally reached the door and walked out into the bright, dry sunlight. Making our way to the curb, we waved our claim checks in the direction of the parking attendants and waited for our cars. Just then, a young woman with a long, brown braid down her back and red-rimmed eyes touched Stacy's shoulder.

"Oh, Stacy. I'm so glad you came. Is Zachary okay? Does he know?" she asked.

"Maggie! Dear, sweet Maggie! Zack's fine, he's doing great. I told him about Abigail, but he doesn't really understand. How are *you* holding up?"

"Um, I don't know. I'm like, totally in shock. You know, we were together until just before it happened," the young woman said, her eyes welling up with tears.

That caught my attention. I immediately butted in on the conversation.

"You poor thing," I said. "You saw her right before she died?"

Stacy shot me a warning glance.

"*Juliet*. This is Maggie Franks. She's one of the teachers in the Billy Goat room. Maggie, this is my friend Juliet Applebaum."

I reached out my hand and shook Maggie's limp one.

"Did you know Abigail?" she asked.

"No, not really," I replied. "I just came to keep Stacy company."

Stacy snorted derisively. I hurriedly continued, "We were heading out for some lunch. Would you care to join us?"

Maggie looked at me gratefully. "You know, I think I would. Mr. Mooney isn't having any kind of reception today, and I really don't feel like being alone right now."

Stacy, who had been glaring at me incredulously, politely seconded my invitation and we arranged to meet at Babaloo, a little restaurant nearby. We retrieved our cars and set off in a convoy. It didn't occur to us to go in one car, but then why would it? This was L.A., after all. Stacy and I each found parking right away and waited in the restaurant while Maggie circled the block, looking for a space.

"What's this all about, Juliet? Why did you ask her to join us?" Stacy asked me.

"Well, she's Zack's old teacher."

"And?"

"And she may have been the last person to see Abigail alive. I just want to find out if she knows anything that might be useful."

"I thought you had decided to give this up after your brawl with LeCrone. I thought we'd agreed that you were going to leave the detective work to the professionals."

"First of all, *we* didn't decide anything, you did." I paused for a moment, distracted by the thought that I'd used precisely the same line on Peter. Giving my lack of originality an inward shrug, I continued, "And second of all, it seems to me that the police have pretty much decided that this is a random hit-and-run. If that's the case, then they're not going to be doing much investigation. And if they aren't, why shouldn't I? I'm trained for it. I know what I'm doing. There's no harm in me looking into things a bit."

"LeCrone might take issue with that point of view." Sometimes Stacy can be downright snide.

At that moment we spotted Maggie's car pulling into a space that had opened up in front of the restaurant.

"Just do me a favor, Juliet. Don't be too pushy with Maggie. She's a real sweetheart, and I'm not sure she can hold her own with you."

"I'm not going to be pushy. When am I ever pushy?" Stacy raised her eyebrows.

"Trust me," I said hurriedly as Maggie walked into the restaurant. "I'll be gentle and restrained."

"You'd better be," she whispered to me, waving her hand at Maggie. "Honey! We're over here!"

STACY ordered her usual—diet fare. This time it was plain grilled fish and a salad with no dressing. Someday I'm going to tattoo "No butter, no oil" onto her skinny butt. Come to think of it, there's probably not enough room. Maggie got something multigrained and sprout-filled. I got a steak sandwich and fries. I didn't really want the fries, but someone had to fulfill our table's daily caloric requirement.

As we sipped our iced teas, I gently directed the conversation back to Abigail Hathaway.

"Maggie, you mentioned that you saw Abigail right before she died?"

So, maybe I wasn't so gentle.

"Yes. No. I mean, not right before. But that evening. After school," Maggie said.

"What time?" I asked.

She looked at me curiously, but answered my question. "About 6:10 or so. After the last late pickup."

Stacy interrupted. "Maggie runs the afternoon day-care program. School ends at one, but some of the kids stay until six."

"Nine to six?" I was surprised. "That's a really long day for a three-year-old."

Maggie nodded. "I think so, too. But we only have a few who stay that late. Most of them go home at three. That's why we have two teachers in the early afternoon, and only I stay late."

"Abigail always stayed with you?" I asked.

"Usually," Maggie said. "She didn't like to have just one teacher there, in case something happened, so she'd do administrative work until the last pickup at six. I don't know who's going to stay late with me from now on." She sniffed loudly as her eyes filled with tears.

Stacy patted her on the hand. "Don't worry, sweetie. I'm sure the new director will stay with you."

I hadn't even thought of that. "Who is going to be taking over the school now?" I asked. "Does anybody know?"

Maggie shook her head. "The board of directors will have to decide. It seems so weird. It's Abigail's school! It's not like they could just hire someone new to take her place."

I turned to Stacy and asked, "Is Heart's Song a nonprofit? Is it run by a foundation or something, or did she just own it outright?"

Stacy thought for a moment. "I'm pretty sure it's like any other private school. It's officially run by a board of directors, although they're just figureheads, really. Abigail made all the decisions. I know it's a nonprofit because I used to deduct all the donations I made every year."

"Unless you were just committing tax fraud," I said.

"Well, if I was, then my accountant was, too. His kids are Heart's Song alumnae."

"Okay, so we're pretty sure the school is going to continue, even without Abigail. The question is, who's going to run it? Who's going to get her job?" I mused.

Maggie gave a little sob. "Oh, no, I hope they don't make Susan Pike the new director. If they do, I'm quitting, I swear."

"Susan Pike? Who's that?" I asked.

Stacy answered, "She was one of the first teachers Abigail hired. She's been there as long as the school's been open. She's kind of an old dragon, but really good with the kids."

"She may be good with the kids, but we all hate her," Maggie said vehemently. "I don't feel bad about telling you that now, Stacy, because Zachary's graduated. The only person who can stand to be around her is Abigail."

"Then I'm sure they won't make her the new director," I tried to reassure Maggie.

"Did anything unusual happen the night Abigail was killed?" I asked, changing the subject. "Did you notice anything out of the ordinary?"

"The police already asked me that. I told them everything was just the same as always."

"So it was just your basic Monday night?"

"I guess so."

"Like every other day of the week?"

"Yeah. Well, no."

"No?" I asked.

"Fridays are different," Maggie said. "On Fridays Abigail leaves at a quarter to six because she's got therapy at six. But on every other day she stays late with me. Just as she did that night." Maggie started to sniffle.

"She was seeing a psychologist?" I asked. It was hard for me to imagine supremely confident Abigail Hathaway in therapy. I'm not sure why, since it seems like everyone in Hollywood is seeing a shrink, but I wouldn't have expected Abigail Hathaway, the frost queen, to regularly unburden her soul. It just didn't seem her style.

"There's nothing wrong with seeing a therapist," Maggie said defensively. "Anyway, she'd only been going for a few months. It's not like she was crazy or anything."

"Do you know who she was seeing?" I asked, not really imagining that Maggie would, or would say so.

"Well, let me think. A couple of months ago the doctor called and canceled the appointment because she was sick. I took the message because Abigail and Susan were having a f—— a discussion. Let me see if I can remember the doctor's name."

"Try. Try hard," I pressed.

"I remember thinking it was Chinese. Tang? Wong? Wang, that's it, Wang!"

"The doctor's name was Wang?" I asked. "Was it a woman? Do you remember the first name?" It couldn't be the same one, could it?

Back when Ruby was first born, and Peter and I were going through our difficult period of adjustment, we had, on the advice of a friend, visited a couples counselor. Peter had had a movie in production just then and he had gotten friendly with the lead actress, Lilly Green, a budding starlet who soon thereafter surprised everyone by winning a supporting-actress Oscar for her first serious film performance. At the time she was shooting Peter's movie, she had been in the process of dissolving her own rocky marriage and gave Peter the name of her therapist, one Dr. Herma Wang.

We'd made an appointment with Dr. Wang, who turned

out not to be the tiny, slim, Asian woman I had been expecting, but rather a somewhat overweight Jewish matron with a thick Long Island accent, who used her married name.

Peter and I had lasted exactly one session with the good Dr. Wang. In the first three of our fifty minutes she'd managed to drop the names of three or four hundred of her most famous patients. Not their last names, mind you. She'd say things like, "As I said to one of my patients, 'Warren, every marriage is a partnership,' " or "As I often tell a patient, 'Julia, you can't expect him to understand you if you don't utilize your three-part communications technique.' "

Technically, I suppose, she wasn't violating anyone's confidences, but really, how many of us *don't* know who those folks are? Peter and I decided that whatever problems we had weren't worth spending a hundred bucks an hour to hear Dr. Wang wax poetic about the trials and tribulations of Mel, Matt, Bruce, and Susan. We never went back.

"Yes, it was a lady doctor, but I don't really remember her first name," Maggie said.

"*Could it* have been Herma?" I asked.

"Maybe. I don't know. Why are you asking me all these questions?"

"Juliet's just a busybody," Stacy said, pinching my leg under the table.

Realizing I wasn't likely to get any more out of Maggie, I stopped the interrogation and kept my mouth shut for the remainder of the lunch. While Stacy and Maggie spent the next half hour or so sharing fond memories of Zachary's years at Heart's Song, I sat and pondered what I had discovered. If Abigail Hathaway was really seeing Dr. Wang, marriage counselor to the stars, then she was most likely going to couples counseling. If she was going to couples counseling, that meant her marriage to Daniel Mooney might be in trouble. And if that were the case, maybe he plowed her into a mailbox! It might be a huge jump from getting a little marital counseling to murder, but as I said before, Daniel Mooney had really rubbed me the wrong way. It wouldn't make any sense *not* to investigate this lead, even if it was a little far-fetched.

The waitress stopped by to clear our plates, and asked us if we were interested in coffee.

"I'll have a double, half-caf, nonfat latte," Stacy ordered.

I thought for a moment. Had I exceeded my caffeine allotment for the day? I decided that I probably had. "I'll have the same. But not a double. And not nonfat. And decaf," I said.

The waitress looked at me, confused.

"A single, decaf latte," I said. "Full-fat."

"Oh. Okay," she replied.

"I don't think I'll have anything," Maggie said. "Actually, I think I'd better get going. I should do prep for tomorrow. It's music day and I want to teach the kids a new song."

Neither Stacy nor I objected. Maggie gathered herself together, kissed Stacy warmly on the cheek, shook my hand coldly, and left.

I watched her walk out the door and, once she had gone, turned to Stacy.

"So, what's the deal, Stacy? What's going on with you and Bruce LeCrone?"

She jerked her head up at me and blanched. "Nothing."

"Baloney."

"Seriously, nothing. Ooh, look, our coffee is here." She

busily engaged herself in pouring copious amounts of artificial sweetener into her tall mug.

"Stacy."

My friend looked up at me. "How did you know?" She whispered.

"I talked to you on Monday night. I even said something like, 'Maybe LeCrone killed her,' and you never mentioned that you saw him that night. You never mentioned the party."

"Didn't I?" She looked pale and almost frightened. "Juliet, promise me you won't say anything. Please. It's over. I swear it's over. It was over as soon as you told me about what he did to his wife."

"What's over, Stacy?"

"Me and Bruce. It was nothing, really. Just a fling. I mean, for Christ's sake, I'm entitled. Do you know how many times I've had to deal with Andy's little adventures? It's about time it was my turn."

Stacy's husband, Andy, has always been a notorious womanizer. Stacy knows it. Her friends know it. Everyone knows it. Every couple of years they separate, only to get back together again a few weeks or months later after therapy and lots of promises of eternal fidelity. I'd thought Stacy had reached some kind of peace with it— that she'd gotten used to it in a way. Maybe she had. Maybe betraying him back was her way of dealing with Andy's treachery.

"How long were you seeing LeCrone?"

Stacy laughed mirthlessly. "I'd hardly call it that. We had sex a few times. The first time was in his bathroom in the middle of a party."

I grimaced. She looked at me, almost defiantly. "We got carried away."

"I guess you did," I said. Then I felt bad about sounding so judgmental. "It sounds pretty exciting."

"It was. I met him a couple more times. And then, that Monday night we got a room at the Beverly Wilshire. That was the last time." She was looking straight into her coffee cup, and it took a moment for me to realize that she was crying.

"Oh, Stacy, honey, don't cry," I said. "You're right, you do deserve it. Andy's been doing this kind of thing to you for years. You are entitled. Really you are."

"But you wouldn't have done it," she said.

That brought me up short. No, I couldn't imagine cheating on Peter. But then, I couldn't imagine him cheating on me, either.

"I don't know, Stacy. I have no idea what I would do under similar circumstances. But that doesn't matter. All that matters is how you feel."

"Well, I feel like I'm the one who was hit by a car."

I reached my hand out across the table, and she took it. We sat there silently for a few more minutes and then paid the bill, gathered our things together, and left. We stood awkwardly in front of my car. I reached out my arms and hugged my friend.

"Call me, okay?" I said when I released her.

"Okay. I love you, Juliet."

"I love you, too. You're my best friend. You know that, don't you?"

"Yeah. I know. You're mine, too."

I waved good-bye, opened my car door, and squeezed myself behind the wheel. I headed for home, thinking about all those terrible marriages around me. LeCrone and his wives. Andy and Stacy. Abigail Hathaway and Daniel Mooney. It often felt like Peter and I were the only happily married couple we knew. Sometimes that made me feel complacent, better than anyone else. Sometimes it just scared me. Maybe we weren't any different. Maybe it was just that our misery simply hadn't started yet.

Eight

I walked in the house and, not hearing Ruby's voice, peeked my head into Peter's office. He was lying on his stomach on the floor, surrounded by *Star Wars* action figures, carefully putting the mask on Darth Vader.

"*Luke,* it is your destiny," I said.

"Hi." He didn't look up.

"Where's Ruby?" I asked.

"Nap."

"Whatcha doing?"

"Playing."

"Hmm."

Peter's "office" looks like an eight-year-old boy's clubhouse. The bookshelves are crammed full of action figures. He's got every comic book hero placed carefully next to the appropriate villains. I'm convinced Peter collects all these toys not, as he insists, because they are valuable (although his collection of vintage '70s Mego Superheroes was once appraised at $4,750), or even as inspiration for his writing, but because as a kid he was deprived of them. His mother did her best, but she just barely managed to support her three children after his father walked out on her. Whatever money she had went to cover the basics, such as food and shelter and, of course, television.

Peter spent his childhood craving the toys he saw on TV. He tells one story that always makes me cry, although he tells it as a joke. One year at Christmas he desperately wanted a GI Joe Frogman. His mother couldn't afford the doll, but she did get him the doll's diving suit. He used a tiny, plastic GI Joe coat hanger for a head and shoulders, and tugged the empty wet suit around a bucket of water. I like to tease him that his next feature will star the archvillain "Hangerman." Every time Peter shows up with another two-hundred-dollar Major Matt Mason figurine in the original 1969 packaging and I want to wring his neck, I try to remember that boy with no dolls.

I walked into the room, straddled his prone figure, and lowered myself onto his rear end.

"Ooph." He grunted. "You weigh a ton, babe. It's like having Juggernaut sitting on my butt."

"Gee, thanks. Come to think of it, I do feel sort of like a fat mutant."

"You're not fat, you're pregnant."

"That's turning into your mantra."

"Yeah? Well, I'll stop saying it as soon as you get over your lunatic obsession with your weight."

"First of all, I'm *never* going to get over that particular lunatic obsession, and second of all, you're no stringbean yourself."

"Oh, yeah?" he said, flipping over under me so that I

was straddling his crotch. He started tickling me in the ribs.

"Stop! Oh, please stop. Please please please." By then I was laughing so hard I was crying. I rolled off of him and onto my side on the floor, curling up into as small a ball as I could—that is to say, not very small. He kept tickling me.

"Peter! Stop it right now or I'm going to pee in my pants! I'm serious!"

That made him quit. He leaned down and kissed me on the mouth, lingeringly.

I won't describe what happened next. Suffice it to say we did what most couples do when they find themselves at home on a lazy afternoon with the kid down for her nap and no laundry to be done.

Afterward, as we lay on the floor of his office, tucked together like spoons—well, like a spoon and a ladle—I reached under me and grabbed a little figurine. "Boba Fett is poking a hole in my back," I said, handing Peter the toy.

Holding the doll puppet-fashion, Peter deepened his voice and said, "May the force be with you!"

"It already was, baby," I said. "Hey, guess where I went this afternoon?"

"Yoga?"

"Nope. Abigail Hathaway's memorial service." I winced, waiting for the boom to drop. Surprisingly, it didn't.

"Hmm," he said.

"That's it? Hmm? Aren't you angry? Aren't you going to tell me to mind my own business?"

"Nope."

"Why not?"

"Well, Juliet, I've been thinking about it a lot. For the past year or so you've been sort of at loose ends. It's like you know you should be staying home with Ruby, but something in you doesn't really like it. You're used to being useful. You're used to helping people. And for some reason, being useful to us, helping your family, isn't as satisfying to you as doing for other people. Ever since you've started looking into this Hathaway thing, you've been different. It's like you've got your old sense of purpose back."

"You know, Dorothy noticed that, too," I said. "I definitely feel like I can contribute something here. But I'm surprised that you're not worried about me."

"Well, I'm not," he replied. "I'm not worried because I know that you know what you're doing. I wasn't worried when you were out canvassing witnesses in Crip or Blood territory. Why should I worry now? I assume that you aren't going to do anything that will put yourself in any danger. I assume that you will nose around and give whatever information you uncover to that detective you spoke to. I assume you'll be sensible."

"I will be sensible. I *am* being sensible, really."

"Good."

"Do you want to hear what I found out at the service?"

"Sure."

"First of all, I saw her husband, who is a total creep. He looks like some Yanni-wannabe."

"Really? That doesn't seem like the kind of person she would be with."

"Exactly what I thought. You should have seen this creep. His stepdaughter was sitting there, weeping, and he barely noticed her. It was awful. I felt like scooping the poor thing up and taking her home."

"I'm glad you didn't. I don't think I could be so under-standing about kidnapping."

"Teenagernapping, actually. She's about fifteen or so. Anyway, it turns out that Abigail was seeing a shrink, and you'll never believe who."

"Who?"

"Herma Wang!"

"Herma Wang, celebotherapist?"

"Wouldn't it be celebratherapist?"

"Celebo is better."

"Whatever. Yes, her! I was thinking I would call Lilly and see if she's still seeing Wang. If she is, maybe she can find out for me whether Abigail was seeing her, too, and if she was, whether it was for couples counseling."

"Lilly's in town," Peter said. "She left a message on the machine this morning. By the way, do we want to stay with her and the twins at the Telluride Film Festival this year?"

"Um, Peter, I don't know if you've noticed, but I'm about to have a baby. I don't thing we're going to make it to Telluride this year."

"Oh, right." He laughed. "I keep forgetting."

"Maybe I'll give her a call and ask her about Wang."

"You do that. I'm going to get back to work," Peter said.

"*Back* to work?"

He blushed. "To work."

"Um, Peter, I found out something else."

"Hmm?" He was already thinking about his script.

"Stacy was with Bruce LeCrone the night of the mur-der."

"At the ICA party. You knew that."

"No, Peter. She was *with* him."

He looked at me. "With as in *with*?"

I nodded.

"Wow. Does Andy know?"

"I don't think so. At least not yet."

"Wow."

We looked at each other and recognized the emotion we were both feeling. Relief. Profound relief to be married to one another. To be married to someone we not only loved, but also trusted.

I kissed Peter and, leaving him to his toys, went to call Lilly from our bedroom. Lilly Green is definitely our most famous friend. She's the only one who's really achieved movie-star status. Despite this, she's managed to stay unpretentious and almost normal. She has the usual Hollywood retinue of personal assistants, business managers, and household staff, but she still drives her twin daughters to school every morning that she's not working.

One of her assistants answered the phone and put me on hold while she checked if Lilly was "available."

"Juliet! Great to hear from you. So, do you guys want to join us at Telluride?" Lilly shouted in the receiver.

"I wish we could, but I don't think we'll be able to manage it with the new baby."

"Oh, that's right, I totally forgot! When are you due?"

"In about a month."

"How fabulous! Boy or girl?"

"A little boy. His name is Isaac."

"That's so sweet! What a terrific name. I can't believe you've picked out a name already. The girls were almost a month old before we'd settled on Amber and Jade. And even then I wanted to change it two weeks later!"

"Well, you know me, decisive to a fault. Listen, I was wondering if you could help me out with something?"

"Sure."

"Remember that therapist you recommended to Peter a couple of years ago? Herma Wang?"

"Of course." Lilly's voice lowered in sympathy. "Do you need her number? Is something going on with you two? Are you okay?"

"No, no, we're fine, it's not that. It's just . . . where do I begin here?" I launched into the long, tangled story of why I wanted to track down the good Dr. Wang. When I'd finished, Lilly whistled.

"Juliet, you are so cool! The crime-solving soccer mom!"

I snorted. "Ruby hasn't started soccer yet. And I haven't solved any crimes."

"I haven't seen Wang as a patient in about a year, but ever since I got my Oscar she's called every couple of months inviting me to lunch."

"How starstruck *is* she?"

"She's pretty bad. It was kind of icky by the end of therapy. She *always* took my side, not that I minded, but it did get a little ridiculous."

"Starstruck enough to breach confidentiality? Could you try to find out if she was seeing Abigail alone, or if she was treating her and her husband, together? And it would be really good to know *why* she was seeing her, okay?"

"I bet I could find out *something* from her. She's so completely indiscreet. I'll take her to the Ivy. That'll knock her onto her butt-kissing butt. This is kind of fun; I feel like Miss Marple!"

"Only much better-looking," I said.

"You flatter me, dahling," Lilly replied, doing her best Zsa Zsa Gabor. "I'll call you as soon as I talk to the doc."

"Great! Talk to you soon."

I hung up the phone just in time to hear Ruby yelling from her bed.

"Mama! Nap all done! Come get me! Mama come *now*!!"

"I'm coming!" I yelled back. "And stop yelling at me!"

I walked into Ruby's room and found her standing in her crib, one leg hoisted over the side.

"What are you doing, Houdini-baby?" I said, grabbing her just in time to break her fall.

"Nap all done," she said. "I want out."

"I see that," I said. "If you're big enough to climb out of your crib, maybe you're big enough to get a big-girl bed. Do you want a big-girl bed?"

"No."

"You could pick one out by yourself."

"No."

"It could be a really pretty bed," I wheedled. I needed to get her out of that crib before her brother made his appearance. No way was I buying a second crib.

"No." *Jeez,* this kid was stubborn. Wherever did she get that?

"It could be pink," I said in a singsong voice.

That sparked her interest. "Pink?"

"Sure. Wouldn't that be great? Let's go buy you a pink, big-girl bed!"

"No."

Time to quit while I was behind. "Okay. Never mind. Let's go find Daddy."

It took all of three seconds to pry Peter away from his work. The bait was a trip to the grocery store to buy the fixings for chicken tacos. The man is easily distracted.

Peter wheeled our big cart down the aisles, Ruby trundled along behind wheeling her minicart, and I brought up the rear, wishing that one of them was wheeling me. In the produce aisle I caught up to Peter and asked, "Do you *goyim* have any ritual where friends and family pay visits on the bereaved after a death?"

"You mean like a wake?" he asked.

"No. Not like a party or anything. More like . . . well, like a *shiva* call."

"What's a *shiva* call?"

"You know, we paid a *shiva* call on my aunt Gracie when Uncle Irving died."

"Oh, right. Of course. When they sat around on stools for seven days and everybody came by with food."

"Exactly."

"Nope. I don't think there's a WASP equivalent."

"Really? That's so cold! You just let the family mope in their house all alone?"

"No, Juliet. We all meet up at the country club and play a round of golf. And then we have a big meeting and discuss how to keep the Jews and blacks out of the neighborhood."

I laughed. "Seriously, there's no time where you just drop by and visit the family?"

"Not really. Although my mom is always dropping off casseroles for eligible widowers. Does that count?"

"No, I don't think . . . wait a minute, maybe that *could* work."

"What could work?"

"Maybe I could make a casserole for Abigail Hathaway's husband!"

"That's a terrible idea."

"Why? I think it's a great idea."

"First of all, didn't you say she had a daughter?"

"Yes. So what?"

"It's hardly fair to leave her an orphan. I can't imagine a surer way to kill the poor girl's stepfather than feeding him a casserole that you made."

"Ha, ha. You're a laugh a minute."

"Seriously, Juliet. You don't even know these people. You can't just show up with food."

"Why not? I'm just showing support. Helping them out. And I did *so* know her."

"You did not. She probably wouldn't even have recognized you."

"Yes, she would have. She would have remembered that you saved her from Bruce LeCrone. And anyway, *they* don't know how well I knew her."

"Juliet, be careful around that family. This isn't a game. They're grieving."

"I will be careful. I just want to get a sense of them, on a more personal level. I'm not even going to ask any questions."

"I'm just giving you my two cents."

"Duly noted. And I will be discreet. I promise." I gave his arm a reassuring squeeze. "Okay?"

"Okay."

"Peter?"

"Yes?"

"How would you feel about cooking up a little casserole?"

"Oh, my God. No. Definitely not."

"Please. Oh, please." I kissed him on the cheek.

"I can't believe you."

I reached out to a grocery bin and tossed a few bags of spinach into our cart.

"What's that for?" Peter asked.

"Spinach lasagna. Only make it with fewer onions this time. Most people don't like as many onions as you do."

Nine

THE preschool gig sure paid well, I thought as I pulled up in front of Abigail Hathaway's oversized Tudor house in the Santa Monica Canyon, one of the most prestigious neighborhoods on the Westside. A manicured lawn stretched from the brass-riveted front door down to the curb. A brick path meandered down the lawn between carefully tended beds of winter flowers. In the driveway were parked two cars—a bright-blue Jeep, and one of those BMW two-seaters that a certain kind of middle-aged man feels compelled to purchase immediately upon seeing James Bond tooling around in one on the silver screen.

Gee, I wonder which car belongs to Daniel Mooney? I thought.

I got out of my suburban-matron heap, careful not to wrinkle the baby-blue maternity smock I had found crumpled at the back of my closet and had actually managed to iron in preparation for my incursion into Mooney territory. I looked innocuous and very, very sweet.

Reaching into the backseat, I grabbed the handles of a shopping bag containing a spinach-and-feta-cheese lasagna that Peter had obligingly whipped up. I walked up to the front door, stretched my face into a sickly sweet smile, and knocked briskly. While I waited for an answer, I reached into the shopping bag and took out the foil pan of lasagna. Without warning and with a sudden jerk, the door opened. Startled, I gave a little jump. Not much, but just enough to tilt the lasagna pan and send a stream of tomato sauce out from under the foil wrapper and all over the front of my smock.

"Oh!" I said with a gasp.

Abigail Hathaway's daughter stood in the doorway. "Oh, no!" she said, reaching out and steadying the pan. "You got it all over yourself!"

I looked down at the splash of red festooning my chest and belly.

"Lovely. Just lovely," I said, ruefully.

"I'm so sorry," the girl said.

"No, no! It's not your fault! Don't be sorry. It's me. I'm just a complete klutz. I'm the one who's sorry." I motioned toward the sauce-covered pan. "This is for you and your . . . your dad."

"Thanks," she said, although she clearly didn't mean it.

"It's lasagna."

"Great." Looking vaguely nauseated, she gingerly took the pan from my outstretched arms.

"Would you like to come in and get cleaned up?"

"That would be terrific. My name is Juliet Applebaum. I knew your mom."

Standing in the doorway, holding a pan of lasagna, Abigail Hathaway's daughter started to cry. She cried not like the grown woman she looked like, but like the child she was. Huge, gasping sobs shook her narrow chest and tears poured down her face. Her nose streamed and, arms filled with lasagna, she turned her head to the side, trying ineffectually to wipe her nose on her shoulder. As she lifted her shoulder to meet her nose, the pan slipped from her hands, falling to the floor with a wet *splat* and spilling tomato sauce over her shoes.

"Oh, no! Oh, no!" the girl wailed, dropping to her knees and trying to stem the tide of sauce making its way across the floor in the direction of a pink and white Oriental floor runner.

I looked around me for a cloth, anything to catch the spill before it ruined what was surely an expensive carpet. Unsurprisingly, there was nothing to be found. I looked down at my shirt, and, with a helpless shrug, whipped it off over my shoulders and, joining Audrey Hathaway on the floor, used it to mop the spilled sauce. She sat back and stared at me, her surprise completely stopping her tears. I finished cleaning up the spill, tossed my filthy shirt on top of the lasagna pan, and hoisted myself to my feet, holding the by now quite disgusting offering in my arms.

"Where's the garbage pail?" I asked.

"In the kitchen. Through there." The girl pointed down the hall. I first checked my shoes to be sure they were clean of sauce, and then headed down the hall toward the perfectly appointed kitchen. I glanced at a gilt-framed mirror that I passed and was horrified to see myself in my black-and-white-spotted maternity bra, the one Ruby likes to call my cow bra. My stomach bulged over the top of my leggings, and my belly button made a little tent in the black fabric. Shuddering, I rushed into the kitchen. I crammed the pan, shirt and all, into the stainless steel

trash bucket under the sink, found some paper towels on
the counter, unrolled a few dozen sheets, and soaked
them with warm water. Carefully squeezing out the towels, I made my way back to Audrey, who was still kneel-
ing in the middle of the entryway. She hadn't moved, but
neither had she resumed her sobbing. I took each of her
hands and gently cleaned them. Then, I wiped the sauce
off her shoes and scrubbed up the last traces from the
floor. I went back to the kitchen, threw out the mess of
paper towels, and returned to the hall. Audrey hadn't
budged.

Groaning, I lowered myself next to her and stretched
my arms out to her. Silently, she inched over to me and
awkwardly leaned into my arms, resting her head on my
chest. She started to cry again, but without the violence
of the first episode. This time her tears fell quickly and
silently, dampening my bra. I rocked her gently, smooth-
ing her hair with my hand.

We sat like that for a few minutes. Finally, Audrey
Hathaway sat up.

"I'm sorry," she said. It sounded like she'd been saying
that a lot.

"Don't be sorry, honey. You have nothing to be sorry
about."

"I miss my mom."

"I know, sweetie. I know."

"You're a friend of hers? I've never met you before."

"Well, no. Not a friend. I met your mother right
before . . . right before she died. My daughter applied to
her school."

She looked at me, still obviously not understanding
what I was doing there.

What *was* I doing there? What had I been thinking? "I
didn't really know your mom at all. She didn't even

accept my little girl to Heart's Song. After I heard what happened I just thought you and your dad might not be that interested in cooking," I finished lamely. I looked around at the devastation I had wrought on her house and on myself.

I couldn't help it. I laughed. Audrey looked startled.

"Look at me!" I said with a gasp through my guffaws.

She seemed to see me for the first time and suddenly burst out laughing, too.

Wiping tears from our eyes, we got up from the floor.

"Can you just see me driving down Santa Monica Boulevard in this?" I asked her.

"You'd probably get arrested!"

"For solicitation! Of cows!" That set us off again.

Once we finally managed to catch our breaths, Audrey stuck her hand out.

"I'm Audrey."

"I know. My name is Juliet." I shook her hand.

We stood looking at each other for a moment and then I remembered something.

"Oh, my God, your father. I can't let him see me like this."

"Stepfather. And don't worry. He's not here."

"You're here alone?" I was astonished. What kind of a man leaves a child alone just days after her mother is killed?

"Yeah. He had to go out. He'll be back soon. Maybe I can find you something to wear."

"That would be great, although I hate to bother you."

We both looked down at my stomach at the same time.

"I guess it would kind of have to be, like, a big shirt or something," she said.

"Like, a really big shirt."

"Wait just a sec, okay?" She ran up the stairs. A

moment later she was back, holding a man's Oxford-cloth, button-down shirt, frayed at the collar and cuffs. I looked at it doubtfully.

"Is this your stepfather's? Do you think he'll mind?"

"It's mine. It used to be my dad's. My real dad. Not Daniel." She spat her stepfather's name out of her mouth as if it tasted bad.

"Do *you* mind if I borrow it?" I asked. "It looks kind of special."

"I don't mind."

"I promise I'll wash it and bring it back tomorrow."

"Okay."

We looked at each other, awkwardly, for another minute. It didn't feel right for me to be there, but I didn't want to leave the girl all alone. Someone had to take care of her, and it was clear that her stepfather wasn't interested in the job.

Audrey reached up and brushed a lock of purple hair out of her eyes. I smiled and said, "I like your hair."

She blushed. "My mom hates . . . hated it."

"I'll bet."

"It's not permanent or anything. It washes out after a while."

"Did you do it yourself?"

"Yeah. I mean, I did the purple part myself. I got the haircut on Melrose." She fingered the shorn side of her head. By now a fine fuzz covered the half that had looked shaved when I saw her at the memorial service.

"Can I feel it? I love the way a buzz cut feels."

She leaned her head over to me and I rubbed my palm across the soft fuzz. "Mmm," I said. "Soft."

She smiled. "Hey, want something to drink? Like tea or something?"

"Sure."

While Audrey bustled around the kitchen putting on the kettle and putting tea bags into pretty ceramic mugs, I perched on a stool at the counter.

"Is there anything you need, honey?" I asked. "Are you doing okay?"

It was a stupid question. She was pretty clearly not doing okay.

"No. I mean, yes. I'm doing fine, I guess. I don't need anything."

For the next fifteen minutes or so I sat sipping tea at Abigail Hathaway's kitchen counter, next to her grieving daughter. Neither of us spoke much, except to comment on the flavor of the tea (peach ginseng) or the weather (chilly, for Los Angeles). There was, however, an odd companionable feeling between us, not like friends and nothing like mother-daughter, but some kind of link nonetheless. Audrey seemed comforted by my presence. Maybe it had nothing to do with me. Maybe the girl was so lonely and so sad that any living, breathing presence would have been enough for her. Whatever it was, by the time I got up to leave, I felt like I had formed a bond with the awkward, sad child.

After my cup had long been empty, I kissed Audrey good-bye, gave her my phone number, and left. As I drove away I turned back to see her standing in the doorway, staring after me. I waved and she lifted her hand for an instant before disappearing into the house.

I drove down the Pacific Coast Highway, onto the Santa Monica Freeway, and into an impenetrable wall of traffic. As my twenty-minute ride stretched to an hour and then some, I had plenty of time to reflect on my actions of the past few days. Investigating Abigail's death had seemed like something I could do. More importantly, maybe, was that it was something *to* do. Meeting Audrey

Hathaway had changed all that. Suddenly I was confronted with what I should have understood from the very
beginning. This was not a chapter out of a Nancy Drew
story. It was a real, live tragedy. Abigail's death was not
an excuse for activity for a bored housewife, but the
worst thing that would ever happen to a teenage girl. How
dare I even attempt to "investigate"? How arrogant of me
to think I was competent to solve this crime! Who did I
think I was, running all over town, questioning nannies,
brawling with studio executives, crashing funerals? I was
deeply embarrassed by my gall in showing up at that poor
girl's house with a Trojan horse in the shape of a spinach-
and-feta lasagna.

By the time I made my way home, I had firmly
resolved to give up my investigative efforts. I decided to
leave it to the people who really knew what they were
doing: the police. I walked in the door, scooped up my
own little girl, and squeezed her as hard as I could. As
Ruby wriggled and howled in protest, I breathed in the
puppy-dog smell of her hair and wordlessly promised her
that I would never leave her like Abigail Hathaway had
left her own little girl. My baby would never ache so for a
mother's touch that she needed to cry in the arms of a
stranger.

I kissed Peter on the cheek and was just about to tell
him about my decision to give up investigating the murder, when he handed me a scrap of paper on which he'd
written the following message:

"Lilly called. Says 'PAY DIRT!' Call her ASAP."

"When did she call?" I asked.

"Just a couple of minutes ago," he replied.

I had to at least find out what she'd discovered. I called
her. The answering machine picked up the phone.

"Lilly? Are you there? It's Juliet. Pick up. I know

you're screening, because Peter says you just called. Pick up pick up pick up pick up pick up."

By now Ruby had joined in and was shrieking "Pick up" and dancing around the room.

"All right, already. For goodness sake!" Lilly's exasperated voice interrupted our song-and-dance number.

"Hi."

"Hi, yourself. Boy, do you owe me. That was the worst lunch of my life. The woman brought a camera and kept asking the waiters to take our picture. By the time dessert showed up she'd taken enough for an entire album."

"I'm so sorry I put you through that," I said with a laugh.

"Doesn't matter. Anyway, do I have some gossip for you!"

"Great!" I said. Then I remembered my decision. "Except I'd sort of decided not to look into this anymore."

"What?!" She sounded genuinely angry. "Do you mean to tell me I withstood two hours of fawning by Herma Wang for nothing? I don't think so, girlfriend."

"I'm so sorry. It's just that I met Abigail Hathaway's daughter, who is in a really bad way, by the way, and I started feeling guilty about playing this Agatha Christie game. I should leave it to the cops, don't you think?"

"Listen, what *I* think is that you are doing this girl a favor. You could find out who killed her mother! You have a civic duty to do whatever you can to help solve this murder. And, moreover, you started this ball rolling, and you should follow it up. At least listen to what I have to say. You can always just call the police and pass the information on to them!"

"I guess you're right. Anyway, I'm dying to find out what Wang told you. I can't believe she really said *anything*. Didn't she take some kind of oath of confidentiality? Does that woman have no ethics?"

"Apparently not. Although it's not like she told me intimate details or even really admitted to treating Abigail Hathaway."

"What *did* she tell you?"

"She said she did have a patient named Abigail, no last name, wink, wink. Wang had been treating her primarily, but she saw the whole family at various points. You were right: Daniel-no-last-name-either and Abigail were having problems—serious ones, according to Wang. She wouldn't tell me what, but she did say that divorce was possible, even likely."

"I knew it. I just *knew* it."

"That's not all. Apparently she also saw the daughter a few times. There were some serious problems there, too."

"I called that, too. I stopped by Abigail's house today and found Audrey, the daughter, all by herself. Her mother *just died,* and her stepfather can't be bothered to keep her company."

"Nasty."

"Yup. Did Wang give you any ideas about what was going on with Audrey and her stepfather? Any abuse or anything like that?"

"She didn't say. All she would say was that the problems they were all having seemed more serious than normal marital difficulties or adolescent angst."

"Lilly, you've outdone yourself. This is all *really* interesting. I'm not sure that it's a motive for murder, but it sure does paint our grieving widower in a different light. I knew the guy was rotten the first time I saw him. And my first impressions are *always* right."

"You know what I like best about you, Sherlock?"

"What, Watson?"

"Your self-effacing nature."

"I *am* modest, aren't I?"

I thanked Lilly for her time and, promising to see her soon, hung up the phone.

"What's this I hear?" Peter said. "Giving up the private-eye biz?"

"Oh, I don't know," I said with a sigh. "I guess so. I started feeling really guilty once I met Audrey, Abigail's daughter. The poor thing cried in my arms today."

"Jeez. I heard what you told Lilly about the stepfather. He sounds like a real creep."

"Totally," I agreed.

Peter, Ruby, and I got up a game of Chutes and Ladders, which I played absentmindedly, all the while trying to decide whether to act on the information Lilly had given me. Every time I landed on the boy stealing cookies or the girl coloring on the wall and had to slide my piece down a chute into a losing position, I felt like someone was trying to tell me something. Finally I decided that the only responsible thing to do was let the police know what I had discovered and leave it at that. Let Detective Carswell do his job.

After losing to Ruby as usual (Peter placed a distant third), I called the detective. I managed, miraculously, to find him at his desk.

"Detective Carswell? This is Juliet Applebaum. We spoke about the Hathaway affair, if you recall."

"Yes, Mrs. . . . er, Ms. Applebaum. I do recall our conversation."

"I have some more information for you."

"Relevant information?"

Was it just to me, or was this guy this sarcastic to everyone he dealt with?

"Yes, *relevant* information. At least I think it's relevant," I answered, trying to keep my own voice as neutral as possible. The detective obviously thought I was a hysterical ninny, and I didn't want to give him any more fuel to add to his snide little fire.

"Why don't you let me be the judge of the information's relevance," the detective said.

I gritted my teeth with irritation. Why is it that a certain kind of man thinks that just because you happen to be a mother you also are necessarily an idiot? In my prior incarnation as a criminal defense attorney, I had grown used to being taken seriously. Very seriously. Prosecutors might not like what I had to say, and they might not be willing to give my clients the deals I wanted, but they never condescended to me. Now, suddenly, just because I had doffed my barrister's wig and donned a housewife's kerchief, people like Detective Carswell thought they could pat me on the head and send me on my way.

"Well, Detective Carswell, how do you judge the relevance of the fact that Abigail Hathaway and her husband were going through serious marital difficulties and, in fact, were considering divorce?"

That got his attention.

"How do you know this? Who told you about this? How reliable is your source?" His sentences tumbled out in a rush.

Well, well, well. Now I was suddenly someone with sources.

"The information is very reliable. Ms. Hathaway and her husband were seeing a marital counselor named Herma Wang. According to Dr. Wang, they were in serious trouble, perhaps enough to lead them to divorce."

"And you spoke to Dr. Wang?"

"No, *I* didn't speak to her. A mutual friend and onetime patient of hers spoke to her and was told about this."

"The psychiatrist discussed the case with your friend?"

"Yes and no."

"Yes and no?"

"Yes, they discussed the case, but Dr. Wang, who's a psychologist, by the way, kept the conversation hypothetical. It was clear who she was talking about, however."

"Clear to whom?"

"To my friend."

"And who is this friend?"

"I'm afraid I can't divulge that information. I promised my 'source' confidentiality."

"Ms. Applebaum, this is a murder investigation. You are hindering the investigation of a murder. Do you understand that?"

That really ticked me off. "Hindering? Hindering? How, exactly, is telling you something that you obviously don't know and can clearly help you, hindering? Precisely the opposite, I would think."

Realizing that the detective was more interested in finding out who my link to Wang was than finding out whether the information I had could provide a clue to what had happened to Abigail Hathaway, I decided to end the call.

"Listen, Detective, I'm not going to tell you who told me about the shrink. You'll have to subpoena me for the information. I'm hanging up now." And I did. So much for passing my information along to the police and letting them figure out what to do with it.

Ten

THE next morning I woke up early and spent the first twenty minutes of my day hunched over the toilet seat, vomiting up not only last night's dinner but also everything I'd eaten in the previous six weeks or so. Why do they call it morning sickness? It's pretty much an all-day affair, and what's worse, it can disappear for months and then suddenly rear its truly ugly head. During my pregnancy with Ruby, I had once been overcome by it on my way to work. There I was, walking up the front steps of the courthouse in my navy suit, holding my Coach briefcase and matching purse. I nodded a grave but courteous good morning to the jurors who were milling about, smoking their last cigarettes before heading inside to decide the fate of my cross-dressing bank robber. A few of them returned my greeting, then recoiled as I proceeded to lean over the balustrade and puke my guts out over the side. I then had the humiliating task of asking the judge to instruct the jurors that defense counsel's tossing of cookies should not be construed as an indication of her confidence in the strength of her client's case.

This time around I threw up with Ruby standing behind me, her chubby arms wrapped around my legs and her head resting on my ample behind. It would have been the greatest luxury to be able to deal with my bathroom business unaccompanied. I couldn't remember the last time I was allowed the extravagance of a closed door.

Cooking Ruby's scrambled eggs almost sent me back to the bathroom, but I managed to restrain myself, cram her into her booster seat, and put her breakfast in front of her. I then tiptoed into my bedroom and retrieved Audrey Hathaway's father's Oxford shirt. I washed it in cold water on the most gentle cycle of my washing machine. I was terrified that I would somehow damage it. I imagined myself standing at Audrey's front door, a shredded piece of stained cloth in hand, explaining to the poor orphan how my spin cycle had eaten her prized possession.

By the time the shirt was dried, fluffed, and folded, Ruby and I were dressed and ready to face the day. I didn't particularly want to take a toddler with me on this errand, but Peter was still sound asleep, and I didn't have much choice. We set off for the Hathaway house.

I pulled up in front of the Tudor palace and looked in the driveway. Both cars were there. Suddenly something occurred to me. Yesterday, when I'd visited Audrey Hathaway, the cars had been in the driveway. Yet, her stepfather hadn't been home. The BMW, however, had to be his. So why hadn't he been driving it? Los Angelenos like Daniel Mooney do not take public transportation or taxicabs. They drive. Moreover, they drive themselves. People don't generally drive one another around. It's not at all uncommon to see convoys of cars following one another as their occupants go to dinner and a movie "together." Maybe Daniel Mooney had *two* cars. Or, maybe, I thought, he had a friend. A very *close* friend.

I unsnapped Ruby's car-seat straps and lifted her out of the car. Together, we walked up the path.

"Are we having a play date, Mommy?"

"No, peachy. We're just dropping something off at this house. Then we'll head over to the park."

"Let's go to the Santa Monica Pier!"

"Not today, Ruby. That's a big outing. We'll do that with Daddy soon."

I glanced down and saw her fat lower lip begin to tremble ominously.

"Ruby," I said, perhaps a bit too sharply, "no tantrums. I'm not kidding. If you throw a tantrum about the pier we're not even going to go to the park."

She mustered up every ounce of willpower in her three-foot body and calmed herself down.

"Maybe we'll go to the pier tomorrow!" she said.

"Maybe. We'll talk about it tonight. Good job holding it together, kiddo."

By then we'd reached the front door. I let Ruby press the doorbell, grabbing her hand after she'd rung it six or seven times. Daniel Mooney opened the door. He was taller than I'd remembered, maybe six-foot-two or so. His long hair was gathered in a ponytail, a style I've never been that fond of, especially when sported by aging men with an outsized sense of "cool." He was wearing a luxurious black shirt in a thick, soft-looking, sueded silk, and I had an almost irresistible urge to stroke it. Ruby had the same idea, and I had to jerk her arm back to keep her from fondling Abigail's widower.

"Yes?" he said. "Didn't you see the sign?" He pointed at the "No Soliciting" sign posted prominently on the door.

"Oh, no, I'm not selling anything. I'm just returning this to Audrey," I said, holding out his stepdaughter's folded shirt.

"Are you a friend of Audrey's?" he asked suspiciously.

"Not really. I borrowed this shirt from her yesterday. I came over to drop off a lasagna and spilled most of it on myself. She lent me this since I had nothing else to wear. I knew your wife." Babbling again. Terrific.

"Oh. You're a friend of Abigail's. Come in." He opened the door and stepped back, making room for me to enter.

"I wasn't really a friend," I said as Ruby and I walked through the doorway. "I knew her from the school. I just wanted to bring something by for you two. You and Audrey, I mean."

Mooney seemed to suddenly notice Ruby. "She's a student," he said.

"No, not yet." I blushed. I decided that now wasn't the time to tell him that his wife had rejected us.

"Please sit down." He motioned toward an archway that led into the formal living room. "I'll get Audrey." He walked up the stairs. I noticed then that he was barefoot and that his toenails sported a decidedly glossy sheen. What kind of a man gets a pedicure?

Ruby and I walked into the elegant living room. The furniture was country French, and the chairs and couches were upholstered in a pale, pink silk. There were end tables everywhere, all of them covered with highly decorative and very breakable knickknacks. I grabbed Ruby just before she could send a collection of tiny music boxes crashing to the floor and sat gingerly in a spindly chair, holding her firmly in my lap.

"Honey, it's too dangerous in here," I said, wrapping her wiggling legs in my own. "I can't let you touch anything. You might break something."

"I *won't*," she whined. "I'll be careful. Please. Please. Please."

"I'm sorry, sweetie."

We were distracted from our wrestling match by Audrey, who came down the stairs wearing blue-and-green plaid flannel pajamas, and rubbing sleep from her eyes.

"We woke you up! I'm so sorry, Audrey."

"That's okay, I've been sleeping a lot lately," she said in a small voice. I inwardly cursed her stepfather for letting her sleep all morning instead of getting her up and distracting her from the depression into which she had clearly sunk.

"I brought back your dad's shirt, honey," I said. "Thanks so much for lending it to me."

"That's okay. Is this your daughter?"

"I'm Ruby. Who are you?" Ruby piped up.

"Hi, Ruby. I'm Audrey." She had crouched down so that she was eye level with the little girl. Audrey clearly had a way with small children. Maybe that was something she inherited from her mother.

"Hey, Ruby, will you thank Audrey for lending Mommy her shirt?"

"Thanks, Audrey."

"You're welcome, Ruby."

"Hey, Audrey, are you okay?" I asked.

"No. I mean, I guess so. I dunno." Her face began to turn a blotchy red, and her eyes filled with tears. Once again, I found myself sitting on the floor holding Abigail Hathaway's daughter while she sobbed. Within moments, Ruby, who hadn't seen that many grown-ups, or almost grown-ups, in tears before, also began quietly crying. I stretched out an arm to my own daughter and rocked them both for a while. I kept looking over Audrey's head in the direction of the stairs, hoping that her stepfather would hear her and come offer his comfort. Nothing. Maybe I'm being ungenerous—maybe he didn't hear her. But why wasn't he there? Why wasn't he with her? Why had he disappeared up the stairs to begin with?

Audrey soon gathered herself together.

"Sorry. I keep doing that to you," she mumbled, extricating herself from my embrace.

"That's okay. At least I didn't spill anything on you this time," I replied.

She smiled politely.

"I think I'm going to go back to bed."

"Honey, do you really want to do that? Isn't there someone you can call to spend some time with you? A relative? One of your friends?" By then I knew enough not to even bother mentioning her stepfather.

"I'm going over to my friend Alice's house this afternoon. Her mom's gonna come get me later."

"Oh, okay," I said, relieved. "Why don't I leave you my number and you can call me if you need anything." I handed her one of my old cards with my home phone number scrawled on it.

I gathered up a still distraught Ruby and headed to the door. Audrey walked me out. She surprised me by giving me a quick, almost embarrassed hug in the doorway. I hugged her back and carried Ruby to the car.

"She's a sad girl," Ruby said as I buckled her into her seat.

"Yes, she is."

"Why is she a sad girl?"

"Well, Peachy, she's sad because something terrible happened to her."

"What happened?"

I dreaded having to say this, but I had no choice. "Her mommy died."

"Did she get trampled by wild-a-beasts?"

"What?" I answered, shocked. "Wild beasts? No. Are you afraid of wild beasts?"

"No, not wild beasts. Wild-a-beasts. Like Mufasa."

The Lion King. Right. Life lessons brought to you by Disney.

"No, Ruby. Her mommy did not get trampled by wildebeests. She died in a car accident."

"Oh." Ruby seemed satisfied by that answer, and I closed her door and walked around to the driver's seat.

I started the ignition and pulled out into the street. I had just stopped at the stop sign at the end of the block when Ruby announced, "We don't have any wild-a-beasts, but we *do* have a car."

I pulled over to the side of the road, stopped the car, and turned to her. "Ruby, I promise you Mommy is not going to die in a car accident." I'm sure there are hundreds of child-development experts who would be horrified that I said that. After all, it is possible that I could die in a car accident. But, the way I figure it, the chances are pretty slim. And, if I do die, Ruby is going to have a lot more serious traumas to deal with than the fact that her mother promised she wouldn't die. Sometimes you just have to tell your kids what you think they want and need to hear and hope for the best.

"Promise?" she asked in a tiny little voice.

"Promise."

"Okay."

"I love you, Ruby. You are my most precious girl in the whole wide world."

I turned around and glanced in my rearview mirror

before pulling into the street. I was just in time to see a car come to a stop in front of Abigail Hathaway's house. I couldn't make out the driver of the cherry-red, vintage Mustang convertible. Curious, I idled at the side of the road.

The door to Abigail's house flew open, and Daniel Mooney bounded out. He loped down the path and fairly leaped into the passenger seat, and the car pulled away from the curb with a screech. I didn't have time to think about what I was doing—I just acted. As the Mustang blew by me I waited a moment and then gave chase.

Ruby and I followed the car all the way down the Pacific Coast Highway to Venice. I did my best to be discreet, keeping one and even two cars between us. Lucky for me, a bright red Mustang is maybe the easiest car in the universe to tail. It wasn't hard to keep my eye on it. Luckily, also, Ruby fell asleep. I'd like to see Jim Rockford engaging in a car chase while handing juice boxes and Barbie dolls back to a demanding toddler. I certainly couldn't have managed it.

Finally, the Mustang pulled up in front of a fourplex on Rose Street. It was one of the *faux* Mediterranean structures that had sprung up all over Los Angeles in the 1930s, all arches, plastered domes, and Mexican tiles. This one looked like it had seen better days, but it retained a kind of blowsy, overdone elegance.

I drove by the Mustang and pulled into a bus-boarding lane at the end of the block. Slouching down in my seat, I angled my rearview mirror so I could see the car. As I watched, the driver's door opened and a woman got out. She was a tall, striking redhead, no more than twenty-five or twenty-six years old. Her hair hung in thick waves down her back, and she wore jeans and cowboy boots. She carried a large leather bag that looked artfully beat up.

Daniel Mooney got out of the passenger side, and the two of them walked into the building. Just as they reached her front door, I saw him grab her hand and press it to his lips. I gasped, although I'm not sure why, because by then I was sure I'd found his paramour and the motive for his murder of the woman I'd by then decided was a martyr in a miserable marriage to a selfish, heartless beast.

I circled the block and made sure I had the number of the apartment building correct. Then I drove quickly back home. I made it in record time.

Peter was sitting at the kitchen table, hunched over a cup of coffee, when I rushed in.

"You just get up?"

He grunted.

"Ruby's asleep in the car. Will you go get her and put her in her crib?"

Grunting again, he got up and went out to get his sleeping child. I poured myself a glass of juice and drained it. Detective work made me thirsty.

Peter settled Ruby down for her nap and came back to his coffee.

"Listen," I said, "do you mind if I run out? I'll be back in about an hour." I waited for him to ask me where I was going.

"Yeah, fine, whatever," he mumbled. A morning person my husband is not.

I paused at the front door, giving him another moment to ask where I was off to. Nothing. I jumped back into my car and sped down the freeway in the direction of Venice.

The parking gods were not on my side. I circled the block twice before I finally gave up and parked in the tow-away zone directly in front of the apartment building. I flicked on my hazard lights, jumped out of the car, and walked quickly to the front door.

There were four buzzers next to the door behind which Mooney and his redhead had disappeared. Below each one was a narrow mailbox. One mailbox had no name tag, one read "Jefferson Goldblatt," and one was marked "Best & Co." Taped above the fourth bell was a small slip of cardstock elaborately decorated with scrolls and flowers in an Art Deco design. The name "N. Tiger" was hand-calligraphed in a luscious purple ink. The red-haired woman had to be N. Naomi. Nancy. Nanette. Nicole. Noreen. Nesbit. Nephertiti. Noodleroni.

I casually looked around to make sure I wasn't being watched. Satisfied that there was no one in sight, I pulled on the little metal door to N. Tiger's mailbox. It was locked. Thinking it hopeless, but somehow not able to help myself, I yanked a little harder. With a tiny shriek of metal the door popped open, only slightly bent. I gulped but, the damage having been done, looked inside the narrow box. At first sight it appeared to be empty, but then I saw a piece of crumpled white paper flattened against the back of the box. I slid my hand inside, and with the tips of my fingers I could just reach the paper. I grabbed it between my index and middle fingers and eased it out. It was a piece of junk mail, one of those cards with the picture of a missing child on the front and an ad on the back. This one was for a dry cleaner. The card was addressed to "Miss Nina Tiger or Current Resident." I had her.

I shoved the card back into the mailbox and closed the little door as best I could. I had bent the latch just enough to make it impossible to shut. I tried jamming the door shut, and when that wouldn't work I opened it up again and did my best to bend the latch in the other direction. I was engaged in this futile and highly illegal activity when the door to the building opened. I jumped, in part because

I was startled and in part because the door smacked me on the hip.

"Sorry," I heard a woman's voice say.

Cringing, I looked up into the face of Nina Tiger. She had brown eyes and a splash of freckles. She glanced at me and started to look away when she noticed what I was doing.

"That's my mailbox. What are you doing?" she demanded.

"Um. Um. Nothing." Quick with the retort as ever.

"Are you going through my mail?" She pushed me aside and reached into her mailbox. She grabbed the door and noticed the latch.

"You *broke* it? Who the hell are you? What's happening here?"

"I did not break anything," I replied indignantly. "I'm just leaving a note for my friend Jeff Goldblatt. I noticed that your mailbox door was open and that . . . that . . . a letter had fallen out of it. I picked it up and put it back for you. I was trying to close the door so that nothing else would fall out when you opened the door on my stomach." I reached for my belly and gave a little grimace of imaginary pain.

She wasn't sure whether to believe me. We looked at each other for a long moment. "You're a friend of Goldblatt's?" she finally asked.

"Of course," I said. "I was dropping off a check, if you must know."

That extra detail seemed to convince her.

"Well, sorry," she said, and brushed by me.

"Apology accepted," I called to her back and followed her down the path. She stopped at her car, opened the trunk, and took out a shopping bag. I walked quickly back to my car and jumped inside. Breathing heavily and more nervous than I'd ever been in my life, I drove off as fast as I could without speeding. I was home within ten minutes.

Peter was in the same position he'd been when I left, although he seemed to have finished the pot of coffee.

"Hi," I said.

"Hi."

"Awake yet?"

"Getting there."

"Ruby still asleep?"

"Isn't she with you?" He looked confused.

"Peter! You put her in bed forty minutes ago."

"I did? Oh, right. Yeah. She's asleep."

"Will you wake up, already, for crying out loud?"

"I got E-mail from your mother last night," he said, changing the subject.

"What? Why is she writing to you?"

"She's been writing to you, apparently, but you haven't answered. She asked me if there's anything wrong."

"I haven't checked my E-mail in ages," I said. "I'll go log on right now."

It took more than ten minutes for all my E-mail messages to download. I hadn't checked my E-mail since the day before Abigail Hathaway died, and I had a huge backlog of messages. E-mail is a big part of my social life. I write regularly to friends from college and law school as well as to my old colleagues at the federal defender's office. I don't think I've spoken to my mother since she got her first laptop with a modem. She spends all her free time surfing the Web, so her phone line is permanently engaged and she communicates exclusively by E-mail.

After I'd finished answering my mail, I logged on to the Web. I was checking out a few of my favorite sites when an idea suddenly occurred to me. I clicked over to Yahoo, input the name "Nina Tiger," and requested a search. It was only moments before I got my results. One hit. I clicked on the icon and found myself looking at a review of a children's book called *Nina Tiger and the Mango Tree*. Probably not who I was looking for, unless the red-haired woman doubled as an exuberant tiger cub.

I leaned back in my chair, rubbed my belly, and considered the situation. If this woman had a computer and spent time on line, I should be able to find her. It was worth a try. I've never been a big one for newsgroups, those message boards of strangers who share a common interest, although at one point, when I was feeling particularly exasperated with my mother, I posted for a while to a group called alt.reddiaperbaby. While it was entertaining for a while to compare stories about socialist summer camp with twenty or thirty strangers, most of whom were named Ethel or Julius, ultimately I got bored. But I remembered how to use Dejanews, the site that digests all the hundreds of thousands of posts to the thousands of newsgroups on topics ranging from alt.misc.parents to alt.dalmations to alt.gunlovers. I clicked over to it, typed in the red-haired woman's name, and ordered a search. Success. I found an E-mail address registered to a Nina Tiger: tigress@earthweb.net. Cute. Crossing my fingers, I asked for tigress's author profile. If she posted to a newsgroup, I would find out.

Tigress, it turned out, was a big-time cyber-geek. Dejanews provided me with listings of her participation in a whole variety of newsgroups. I checked out her postings to alt.postmodern—tigress was not a fan of Jeff Koons. She did, however, enjoy *Star Trek: The Next Generation* and French cooking. I scrolled down past postings to those groups and others, including one dedicated to the Rajneesh and another whose topic I couldn't figure out—it had something to do with witchcraft, or rugby. One of the two. Then I found something interesting: Tigress spent a lot of time chatting with folks on the topic of alt.polyamory. That sounded like sex to me.

I clicked on tigress's most recent posting to the newsgroup. The protocol of newsgroup participation is to include a portion of the person to whom you are responding's message at the top of your own so that readers will know what the topic of conversation is. Otherwise it would be almost impossible to follow the train of various comments and responses. Tigress had excerpted a prior message from someone named "monkey65" and responded to it.

> <<*Given tigress's frequent lambasting of this poor woman, I'm not sure why we are all expressing sympathy for her loss. IMHO, she didn't lose jack other than an impediment to her relationship with Coyote. He deserves our support, but she certainly doesn't.*>>

> *My loss is immeasurable because my love's loss is immeasurable. I feel his misery in my own soul. His wife's refusal to embrace our love and make it part of her own doesn't ease the pain of her being violently thrust from this life into the next passage. I ache with Coyote as I love with Coyote. Our intertwined souls feel this wrenching together as we feel all else together. We will celebrate her voyage into the next life with a tantric love dance.*
> *tigress*

It was difficult to keep myself from gagging. I wasn't sure what made me more sick to my stomach: Nina Tiger's pretentious, New-Age pseudomourning, or the idea of Daniel Mooney—it had to be he—performing a "tantric love dance," whatever the heck that might be.

I snipped the message and copied it into a file on my computer. In the interests of security, however paranoid, I labeled the file "Animal Musings." No way a hacker, police detective, or nosy husband would figure that out.

I then went back to Dejanews and searched for more information on my pair of tantric murderers. After about an hour I could stand no more. My back ached, my eyes were blurry, and I was thoroughly disgusted. I logged off, put my computer to sleep, and staggered out to the kitchen. I found Peter just where I'd left him. He was still hunched over his empty cup of coffee but seemed to have progressed through all the various sections of the *Los Angeles Times*. The Trades were spread out in front of him, and he was busily circling items with an angry red marker.

"Hey. Whatchya doing?" I asked.

"Figuring out who's getting paid more than I am."

"Oh, for Pete's sake, Pete, tell me you're not serious."

"Totally," he said, miserably. "The *Hollywood Reporter* has this long article on some twenty-eight-year-old hack writer who just turned down one point seven million dollars to write the script for *Revenge of the Killing Crows*. Turned it down. Meaning, it wasn't enough money. Meaning, he's planning on making *more* money doing something else."

"You don't know that. Maybe the guy has some artistic integrity and doesn't *want* to write the *Killing Crows* thing," I said.

"Give me a break, Juliet. First of all, this is Hollywood. No one has artistic integrity. And even if they did, they wouldn't for one point seven million dollars. And second of all, I would *kill* to write the movie that you seem to think is so artistically bankrupt." He positively snarled at me. My sweet, unflappable spouse had turned into a character from one of his own scripts.

"What has gotten into you this morning?" I asked, trying to keep my own temper. For some reason, my moods always seem to adjust to match Peter's. When he's depressed, I'm depressed. When he's angry, I'm angry. Unfortunately, his positive emotions don't seem anywhere near as contagious.

Peter moaned, reached over, and hugged me. "I'm sorry, sweetie. I'm being a bear. I was up until four in the morning trying to finish that scene I'm working on. I am never going to finish this script. Which means I'll never get another movie."

Suddenly he dropped his arms from around my neck and looked at me, horrified. "Oh, my God, do you think *I'm* the reason we've been rejected at all the preschools? They know I'm going nowhere, and they don't want their precious kids to associate with the spawn of failure."

I rolled my eyes. Before I could express a reassuring word, Peter started scrambling around the table.

"Where's a pencil? I have to write that down. *Spawn of Failure.* Great title."

Laughing, I kissed the top of his head. "I love you," I said.

"Love you, too. What have you been up to all morning? How's the baby doing?" He scribbled on a corner of the newspaper and then leaned over and gave my belly a kiss.

"Isaac and I are fine. We were just . . . um . . . driving around."

"What?" he asked. "Driving around?"

"I mean, Ruby and I went to Abigail Hathaway's house to return the shirt to her daughter, and after I dropped her off at home I ... I ... I just drove around." I paused. "I'm lying," I said.

"What?"

"I didn't want to tell you what I really did, so I lied. But I can't lie to you. I did go to Ms. Hathaway's house. But, then, I sort of followed Daniel Mooney."

"You *what?*"

"I followed him. But listen, here's why—"

"I don't care why!" By now he was yelling. "You took our two-and-a-half-year-old daughter on a car chase?"

I yelled back, "It wasn't a car chase! We very slowly and carefully followed Daniel Mooney and his *girlfriend* to her house, and then I immediately brought her back here before I went back to figure out the girlfriend's name. Do you honestly think I would ever risk Ruby's safety?"

Peter paused. "Girlfriend?"

"Yes, girlfriend. And you'll never believe the stuff I found out about the two of them on the Web."

Peter was interested despite himself. "Go on."

"Turns out this creep is sleeping with this woman, Nina Tiger, or "tigress," as she likes to call herself. They met about a year ago on a newsgroup for people interested in polyamory."

"Poly what?"

"Love relationships among more than two people."

"Ick."

"My feelings exactly. Anyway, they met on the Web, and pretty soon were having very public and very raunchy Internet sex. Finally, it wasn't enough for them. They decided they needed to consummate their cybersex. The whole time, mind you, they kept the entire population of their newsgroup apprised of every single sordid detail of their relationship. They started sleeping together, sneaking around behind Abigail's back.

"Within a couple of months, the newsgroup freaks started hounding them. Remember, the whole point of this movement or whatever it is is that they are supposed to by polyamorous, not just adulterous. Tigress and Coyote—yes, that is indeed his *nom de guerre*—finally succumbed to the pressure and decided to include Abigail in their little love nest or cesspool, whatever you want to call it. And, get this, they decided, with the help of their comrades in arms—and legs, for that matter—that the best way to get Abigail to go along with this multiple-partner thing is to have her walk into her bedroom one fine day and find ol' tigress and Coyote waiting there, buck naked."

"Are you kidding?"

"Nope. They planned their moment, and one fine evening there they were, waiting for Abigail when she walked in from work. Surprise, surprise, Abigail was less than thrilled with the little *Wild Kingdom* tableau awaiting her. In fact, she freaked out—which, by the way, totally confused everyone in the newsgroup, all of whom apparently were under the impression that she would rip off her clothes and jump into the sack with the fabulous twosome.

"Not one to be trifled with, Abigail threw Coyote out on his butt, and he, bizarrely, to my mind, began this desperate siege to try to get her back. Finally, after about a week or so of flowers, phone calls, etc., she relented, on the condition that he stop seeing tigress and get some marital counseling, which he did. Go to therapy, that is. He did *not* stop sleeping with the hungry jungle cat. They just went back to doing the nasty in secret. They seem to have been under the impression that Abigail didn't know about it, or at least that's what they told the newsgroup."

"Holy cow."

"Cows say 'Moo!' " a high-pitched voice squealed.

Peter and I spun around to find Ruby standing in the doorway. How long she'd been there and how much she'd heard we never did figure out. I didn't have time to mention to Peter that Nina Tiger had caught me going through her mail.

Eleven

So Daniel Mooney had killed his wife for the second-oldest reason in the book: love. Something still bothered me, however: This was a full thirty years after the "me decade" and the divorce revolution. By conservative estimates, one in every two marriages doesn't make it. Why didn't Daniel Mooney just divorce his wife and marry his trophy, like most other philandering husbands? Why did he kill her, exposing himself to the possibility of taking up residence on San Quentin's death row?

There were two possible explanations that occurred to me. The first had the benefit of a little drama and just a hint of Jacqueline Susann. Mooney, acting in the heat of his overwhelming passion, overcome with lust and despair, struck out in a blind rage. Since Mooney seemed about as capable of passion as your average android, I could pretty much rule that possibility out. That left me with the single biggest motivator of all, the reason most crimes are committed to begin with. Filthy lucre. Money.

That night, after I put Ruby to bed and after Peter had gone to work, I went back to my computer. I logged on to a legal search engine that I'd been subscribed to while at the Federal Defender's office. Surprisingly, my password still worked. Promising myself that I would notify Marla Goldfarb that she should adjust the office's subscription to exclude me and any other ex-employees just as soon as I was done, I began a search of the real property files.

Real property means just that—land, houses, apartments, and the like. The search engine listed appraised values and title histories of all pieces of real property in most if not all areas of the country. In the California real estate market, average, and even not so average, wage earners have the vast majority of their assets tied up in their homes. One of the best ways to figure out what someone is worth—one of the only ways, unless you're the FBI or the IRS and can subpoena bank records—is to figure out what kind of money she has invested in her house.

It took me no time at all to find Abigail Hathaway's property interests. In addition to her house in Santa Monica, she owned eight rental units in East Los Angeles and three small apartment buildings in South-Central L.A. and Watts. Lovely, elegant Ms. Hathaway was a slumlord. Slumlady? Anyway, she collected rent on a number of buildings in decidedly dicey parts of Los Angeles. She also owned a commercial building on Wilshire Boulevard and a couple of empty lots downtown. A real estate magnate in preschool teacher's clothing.

Scrolling down through the document that my entry of her name had generated, I found another listing—a large holding on the central California coast. A ranch, most likely, since it listed agricultural uses under its property description. Old California families often used to own vast ranches all over the state. William Randolph Hearst's San Simeon is the most famous of these, but families such as the Hewletts, Packards, Browns, and others still keep their "rustic" family retreats. It appeared that the Hathaways were part of that select group.

Now the question became how Abigail Hathaway had come into these various properties and what kind of stake, if any, Daniel Mooney had in them.

Before I continued my search I got up and tiptoed into the hall. I paused outside of Peter's office and listened to the rapid-fire click-clack of his computer keys. His work was obviously going better. I continued down the hall and stopped outside of Ruby's door. Opening it a crack, I peered into the semidarkness. She lay on her bed, arms and legs spread wide. That child sure knew how to take up space. Smiling at the sound of her snores, I softly closed the door and headed to the bathroom. The minute dimensions of my pregnant bladder were having a detrimental effect on my stamina.

Business accomplished, I headed back to my desk. Thankfully, I had not been logged off in my absence. Going back to my search, I began with the Santa Monica house. According to the record, it had been purchased in 1983 by Abigail Hathaway and Philip Esseks. 1983. I did some quick math. (Okay, not so quick, but I'm a product of the new math of the early 1970s, and it is simply not my fault that I need to add and subtract using my fingers and toes. And let's not even talk about my times tables.) Sixteen years ago. Abigail's daughter Audrey looked to be about fifteen years old or so. That made it likely that Philip Esseks was Audrey's dad and one of Abigail's first few husbands.

Married couples generally purchase residential property as joint tenants. That means each has a right of survivorship. If one dies, the other owns the whole thing. The house was Abigail's. Even more interesting, there was no bank lien on the property, meaning that it had either been fully paid for when bought or the mortgage had been paid off.

Since Abigail owned the house before her marriage to Mooney, the house was hers and hers alone. Under California's community property laws, each person retains ownership of whatever assets he or she brings into the marriage. It's only what they earn or acquire during the time they are together that gets split down the middle. The house belonged to Abigail, and unless she had expressly made it part of their community property (something I couldn't see a woman who'd been through a divorce or two doing), if Mooney divorced her, he wouldn't get any of it.

I then checked the house's appraised value. Scrolling down, I let out a long, low whistle. Wow. Here was the reason Peter and I would never be able to buy a house in a place like Santa Monica. Abigail's admittedly lovely but certainly not palatial home was appraised at 2.1 million dollars. Yes, you read that right: 2.1 million. And that was only the appraised value. Who knows what she could have sold it for on the open market?

So much for the house. I clicked over to the central coast property. The line of title on that was even simpler. The property had been purchased in 1914 by Alexander Hall Hathaway. It was now owned by the Hall Hathaway Family Trust, with Abigail Hathaway listed as trustee. The ranch's appraised value was a cool twenty-six million dollars. Good news for Abigail, but meaningless to Mooney. Inherited property is not subject to the community property laws. He would have gotten none of it had they divorced. Presumably, however, he wouldn't get any part of it at her death, either. I was pretty confident that the ranch would go to the Hathaway heir—Audrey.

The only thing left to figure out was the ownership status of the commercial holdings—the various apartment buildings and lots sprinkled throughout town. It took me a while, but I finally managed to figure out who owned what. It appeared, curiously, that Abigail was the sole owner of each of the rental units and of the vacant lots. The commercial building on Wilshire Boulevard was owned by an entity called "Abigail Hathaway Ltd.," a limited partnership. Clicking over to the business listings, I entered the name "Abigail Hathaway Ltd." and, after a short wait, came up with a description of the partnership. Its sole member was Abigail Hathaway herself.

I returned to the property screens and spent some time trying to figure out the chain of title of the various buildings. They were all sold to Abigail Hathaway between 1989 and 1995. Interestingly, all the properties except the Wilshire office building and one of the empty lots had been sold to Abigail by the same entity, Moonraker, Inc. Moonraker—it had to be Daniel Mooney.

I tried to figure out who, exactly, constituted Moonraker, Inc., but found myself lost in a tangled web of owners, partners, lienholders, and the like. Finally I gave up. I needed someone with real experience in the field to help make sense of what I'd found. I carefully downloaded all the relevant documents and put them into my Animal Musings file.

It was only once I'd logged off, and put my computer to sleep, that I realized how sore my neck was and how my back ached. I stretched my head from side to side and cracked my neck. Detective work was exhausting. And it made me hungry. I waddled to the kitchen and made myself a bowl of ice cream. I added a dollop of butterscotch sauce and a squirt of whipped cream. I was about to return the whipped cream canister to the fridge when I had a sudden, irresistible urge: I leaned my head back, opened my mouth, and sprayed it full of whipped cream. Coughing and swallowing, I took my light snack to bed.

Twelve

THE next morning, after I'd fed Ruby and settled her in front of *Sesame Street,* I sat at the kitchen table and tried to think of someone who could help me figure out the meaning of what I'd discovered the night before. I needed a real estate lawyer. Fortunately, one of the benefits of going to Harvard Law School is that my old friends and classmates are successfully employed all over the country in good law firms, and, generally, when I need some legal advice, it's easy to find. Unfortunately, in this particular instance, I could come up with only one name: Jerome Coley. Jerome had come to Harvard Law School via the governor's office in Sacramento, where he'd been one of the youngest press secretaries ever to hold the position. Before that he'd been a linebacker for Stanford's football team and had been named All-American two years in a row. He was a complete hotshot. After graduation, Jerome had taken a job in Los Angeles at a prominent local firm and, as I recalled, specialized in real estate law.

There was, however, a slight complication: Jerome had been my boyfriend throughout my second and third years of law school, although our relationship never got as serious as it might have. We just weren't meant to be. He was one of those guys whose ambition is palpable. He knew exactly what he was going to do with his life. He told most people that his goal was to be a senator from the state of California. He confided in me his real dream: to be president. I didn't have much doubt that he'd succeed.

Jerome had his whole life planned out. After establishing himself in the legal community, he intended to run for Congress, serve a few terms, and then make a play for the Senate seat. A white wife didn't figure into his plans. Jerome believed that Californians would have a hard enough time electing a 6-foot-6, 280-pound black man to office without the added benefit of a 5-foot-tall Jewish wife standing proudly at his side. He was probably right.

Anyway, after we'd broken up he'd met and married a sweet young woman of the correct race, the daughter of friends of his parents. We hadn't spoken since our final blowout in the middle of commencement ceremonies (I'd accused him of being a calculating son of a bitch, and he'd responded by accusing me of using our relationship as a sop to my white, liberal guilt), and I wasn't sure how he'd react to a phone call from me. But no matter how hard I racked my brain, I could not come up with a single other real estate lawyer. I had no choice but to give Jerome a call.

I telephoned information, got the name of his firm, and dialed the number before I had time to change my mind. The receptionist put me through to him.

"Jerome Coley." He answered his own phone.

"Hi, Jerry. You'll never guess who this is."

"Juliet Applebaum." There wasn't even a pause!

"Wow. You recognized my voice after all this time!"

"I'd never forget your voice. How you doing, baby?"
Baby?

"Um, okay, pregnant. Again."

"Really? I'd heard you had a kid. Girl, right?"

"Right. Her name is Ruby. This one's a boy."

"Ruby. Pretty name. Is she as beautiful as her mama?"

"Well, since her mama weighs about three hundred pounds right now and has ankles the size of soccer balls, I'd say she's definitely more beautiful."

"I can't believe that. You always look good. Even fat, you'd look good."

This conversation was unbelievable. With a little shiver I remembered how Jerome had always made me feel. Kind of like a melted ice-cream cone. Pulling myself together, I quickly redirected the conversation.

"So you're not mad at me anymore?" I asked.

"Of course not. Are you still mad at me?"

"Of course not. Bygones and all that."

"Right. So you calling to ask forgiveness, or is there some ulterior motive up your adorable little sleeve?"

I laughed. "You still know me a little, don'tcha, Jer."

"Yes, I surely do."

"Well, I do have an ulterior motive, but first tell me how you're doing. How's Jeanette? Do you guys have any kids yet?"

"She's fine. She's been home for the past year and a half with our twin boys, Jerome, Jr., and Jackson."

"Twins? Wow! You must be exhausted!"

He laughed the deep, rolling chuckle that I remembered so well.

"Indeed. Indeed we are."

"And your job, Jer? How's that going?"

"Just fine. I made partner last year."

"I'm not surprised." I wasn't. He was a smart guy, and more importantly, he had always been a team player.

"Congratulations. That's terrific."

"And, Juliet, you probably won't be surprised to hear that I'm running for Congress next fall. Richard Baker is stepping down, and I'm going to be running for his seat."

"Now, that's what I expected to hear!" I said. "I figured it was about time for you to be heading to Washington."

"You know the plan, girl. You know the plan."

We both paused, considering for a moment that, but for "the plan," there was a good chance we would be living together right now, making little *café au lait* babies of our own. Ah, well, such is life. We were both happily married, at least I was, and the better off for our breakup.

I decided to get down to business. "Jerome, I have a couple of questions about a series of real estate transactions that I've been looking into, and I wonder if you might be able to give me some help."

"Of course, baby."

Baby again. He used to call me that in that same deep, sweet voice while we made love. Over and over again. Steeling myself, I got my mind out of the gutter and into the present and concentrated on my questions.

"Okay. First of all, do you have any idea what Moonraker, Inc., is? Have you ever heard of them?"

"Moonraker. Moonraker. That rings a bell. Hmm." He paused for a moment. "I think I remember something about that company. Hold on a second, let me check a file."

He put me on hold long enough for me to get a little too involved in a fond recollection of the past.

"I'm back. I just checked with a colleague. I thought

I'd remembered that name. Moonraker played a small role in a series of deals the firm did in the mid-eighties or so. Things got a little ugly when the market went bust in 1989, and we haven't done any work with them since. They might have gone under. A lot of smaller companies did back then."

Pay dirt.

"Do you happen to remember the name of the principal owner of Moonraker?"

"I didn't, but my partner did. He told me that it was owned by a guy named Mooney. Hence the name. Cute."

"Daniel Mooney?"

"He didn't say. Maybe. Are you doing some kind of deal with Moonraker? Is he back in business?"

"No, nothing like that. Tell me, can you think of a reason why Moonraker would sell off its properties?"

"Well, that's a no-brainer. Real estate transactions are highly leveraged. That means everyone borrows heavily to make each deal. If enough of its deals fell through to force Moonraker to go under, it would have to sell off its assets to pay off its debt."

"That makes sense. Now, can you think of a reason why Moonraker would sell its assets to Mooney's wife?"

"Interesting. Well, maybe Mooney wanted to protect his properties from creditors and was under the impression that if he made them the personal property of his wife they would be exempt from dissolution and distribution. That would have been a mistake on his part, however. You can't protect property just like that."

"Why not?" I asked. I didn't do that well in property law.

"Well, think about it, baby. If you could just sell off your assets to your family, no creditor would ever get anything when a business went bankrupt."

"Oh, right. Then why did he do it?"

"Maybe his wife bailed him out. That's the only thing I can think of. Maybe his wife bought his properties to give him the cash to pay off his creditors. Does she have that kind of money?"

"I think she must have." Abigail Hathaway had the money to pay off her husband's debt, but instead of giving it to him, she bought his properties. So she ended up owning everything and he ended up owing her for the rest of his life.

"Juliet, what's your interest here? Who are you representing?"

"Nobody. I'm not representing anybody. I'm just, well, I'm just sort of investigating a murder."

"You're *what?*"

"Abigail Hathaway, Daniel Mooney's wife, was killed last week. I knew her and I'm sort of trying to figure out who killed her."

"You know, I always thought you'd make a good cop. So you think this guy Mooney killed her and you're going to cuff him and bring him in."

"Ha, ha. Very funny, Jer. I'm not cuffing anybody. It's just that the cops have decided that this is a hit-and-run, which it may well be. Nonetheless, I think it's worth an extra look. I've been spending a little time nosing around. I think you've helped me discover something pretty important."

He laughed again. "Juliet Applebaum, private eye. Hey, girl, don't go getting yourself into any trouble."

"You know what, I kind of like the sound of that: Applebaum, P.I. Anyway, don't worry, I'm not getting into any trouble. And, Jerome?"

"What?"

"Thanks. You've been a great help."

"You're welcome, baby. Anytime."

"Watch out or I'll take you up on that. Regards to your wife and sons."

"Good luck with your new baby, baby."

Now it was my turn to laugh. I said good-bye, thanking him again for his advice, and hung up the phone.

I sat for a moment, staring into space, indulging a brief but nonetheless highly disconcerting fantasy about Jerome and the lazy afternoons we used to spend in his studio apartment in Cambridge. I had fond, very fond, memories of the god-awful, green shag carpeting. It was made out of some horrible acrylic and once gave me such a bad rug burn on my rear end that I could barely sit for a week. With a shiver, I realized that there was only one way I was going to exorcise the demon of Jerome Coley. After checking to make sure that Ruby was still busy with the number 16 and the letter R, I snuck into my bedroom and woke up my husband. Substituting reality for fantasy turned out to be just what I needed.

AFTER I had successfully reminded myself that I was happily married, Peter and I took a quick shower together. I grabbed a pink razor that was sitting in the soap dish and tried to shave my legs. I leaned over and, about halfway down toward my knees, I got stuck. I couldn't bend over far enough. I looked up at my husband, who was rinsing the shampoo out of his hair.

"Um, honey?" I said beseechingly, holding the razor up to him. "It's that time again."

"Really? Already? Last time you could shave your own legs up until the last couple of weeks," he said with a laugh.

"Well, I'm just fatter now, if you don't mind."

"All right, prop your leg up here."

Groaning with the effort, I balanced my leg on the side of the tub. Peter bent down under the spray of the shower and delicately and carefully shaved my leg clean. I reached over and wiped the streaming water out of his eyes. What I really wanted to do was kiss the top of his head, but I couldn't reach it. What a lovely man. How many guys do you know who would shave their pregnant wife's legs? I know exactly one. And I married him.

Suddenly, with a crash, the bathroom door burst open. Peter and I both jumped, and I felt a sting as the razor sliced into my shin.

"Ow! Dammit!" I hollered. "Ruby! What in heaven's name are you doing?"

"Nothing!" she wailed. "I'm lonely!" I ended up crouched on the bathmat, soaking wet and dripping blood and water, trying at the same time both to dry off and to comfort a righteously indignant toddler.

Thirteen

PETER did me a favor and took Ruby out for the rest of the morning so I could do a little more research. I noodled around on the Internet for a while, trying to see if I could come up with some more dirt on either Daniel Mooney or his feline friend. After an unsuccessful hour or so, I was getting very frustrated. Looking at my watch, I realized that if I rushed, I could make my prenatal Yoga class. I definitely needed to clear my head, and moving my body probably wasn't a bad idea. I hoisted myself out of my chair, waddled into my bedroom, and began the arduous process of cramming my body into my maternity Yoga cat suit. Getting my thighs into that Lycra outfit was an awful lot like stuffing a sausage casing.

I was stuck somewhere between my knees and my butt when the phone rang. I lunged over to the nightstand, and fumbling for the phone, knocked the receiver onto the floor. I spent a couple of frantic seconds on my hands and knees, tangled in my leggings, trying to reach under the bed where the receiver had rolled. Finally, I managed to herd the dust bunnies into a corner and answer the phone.

"Yeah? Hello?" I was panting from exertion.

"Um, hello? Juliet? Are you okay?"

"Yeah, fine. I'm fine. Who is this?"

"It's Audrey. Audrey Hathaway. Abigail's daughter. I'm sorry. I hope it's okay to call you. I mean, you said I could call but you were probably, like, just being nice or something. I shouldn't have called. Forget it. I'm—"

"Audrey! I'm so glad to hear from you," I interrupted her. "Of course you can call. I wanted you to call. Are you okay? Why are you calling? I mean, it's fine, but is there something wrong?"

"No. Yes. I dunno." And she started to cry. I sure had a calming effect on that girl.

"Honey, shh. It's okay, sweetie. Are you just sad? Is that it?"

"No." She hiccuped. "I mean, yes, I'm sad, but that's not why I'm calling. I'm totally freaking out here and I have no one to talk to and then I found your number and you're so sweet and I thought you maybe might be there because you're, like, pregnant and can't go anywhere anyway." With that, she began to wail.

I looked down at my legs, still trapped in Lycra. She wasn't far wrong—I certainly didn't give the appearance of anyone who should be leaving the house.

"Should I come over? Do you want me to come over?" I asked.

"No!" she shouted. "No! Not here!"

"Can I meet you somewhere? Do you want to come over to my house?"

She was sitting in my kitchen, drinking hot chocolate, within twenty minutes.

* * *

I let Audrey sit quietly for a little while, slurping cocoa and eating cookies. Her multicolored hair was shoved into a baseball cap, and she was wearing an oversized sweatshirt and a pair of pants so big they looked like I could climb into them with her. I wasn't sure if she was pathologically ashamed of her body, or just expressing the height of a teenage fashion I was too clueless to even know about. Finally Audrey squared her shoulders and seemed to make some kind of decision.

"If I tell you something, like absolutely, totally insane, will you swear that you won't think I'm crazy?"

"You're not crazy, Audrey."

"I know I'm not crazy. I just don't want *you* to think I am."

"I won't. I don't. What is it?"

"The cops are, like, all over my house and they won't tell me why, but I think I know."

"You do?" Did she? Could she know about her stepfather?

"Yeah. It's Daniel. I know it is. He killed my mom. I'm so completely sure he did it." She wasn't crying anymore. She seemed grim, and certain, and scared.

"Your stepfather? Are you just guessing, or do you have proof?"

"Well, it's not like he's confessed or anything. It's just that he hates me and my mom. He left once, you know. He was having an affair, and my mom threw him out."

I decided that it was better to play dumb. "An affair? Really? With whom, do you know?"

"I don't know her name or anything. But I know that he met her online, how lame is *that?* He's like some pathetic old man having *cybersex.* It's so totally gross." Audrey no longer sounded upset. Just really angry.

"How did you find out about this?" I asked.

"My mom made him go to therapy and the two of them dragged me with them a couple of times. So we could 'deal with our family issues.'" Her voice dripped sarcasm. "They were supposed to be talking about me, but my mom ended up screaming about his computer slut. The shrink made her shut up, but I heard enough to figure out what the creep was up to."

"Creep is right," I agreed. "Audrey, I think you should be telling this to the police. Don't you?"

"No! No way. He'll kill me if he finds out I told on him." She started to cry again.

It occurred to me that she might be right. Kill her, as in really kill her, not just be angry enough to ground her for the weekend.

"Okay. Okay. Do you want me to tell the police, and leave you out of it?"

"Would you? Would you do that?"

"Of course, honey. Of course I will. But what are you going to do? You can't go home, can you?" I reached my arm around her and hugged her. I tried to imagine Peter's face when I told him that I'd invited Abigail Hathaway's daughter to stay with us until I could prove that her stepfather was a murderer. I opened my mouth to invite her to stay, but she spoke first.

"I can stay at my friend Alice's. I was going to do that anyway, at least until my aunt comes back. My aunt was here for a couple of days, but then she had to go home. She's coming back soon, that's what she said. She wants me to go live with her in New Jersey, but I don't know if I want to. I mean, who the hell wants to live in New Jersey?"

"I'm from New Jersey," I said, smiling and trying to cut the tension a bit.

"Oh. Sorry."

"Don't worry about it. It's not so bad, New Jersey. But what about school? Don't you want to stay in your school?"

"To hell with school. I'm flunking out anyway. Who cares?"

I didn't want to touch that. The weeks following her mother's death were not the time to lecture Audrey on the importance of an education.

"Okay, you go to your friend Alice's and I'll call the police and tell them what you told me."

"But don't mention my name, okay? Tell them you heard about it from, like, anonymous sources or something."

"I'll tell them something."

I packed a Baggie with some cookies for Audrey. She swore to me that she was going right over to Alice's house, and left the number for me. Then I called Detective Carswell's office and left an urgent message for him to call me.

Checking my watch, I realized that I had a few more minutes before Ruby and Peter were likely to get home. I contemplated getting back onto the computer, but decided that I needed help if I was going to get any more information on Mooney. I decided to call in yet another favor. I dialed the federal defender's office and asked to speak to Al Hockey.

"Hey, it's the Old Woman Who Lived in a Shoe! Have you figured out what to do with all your children?"

"Ha. Funny, Al. Two. Exactly two children. One and a half, really. Less than you, I might add."

"Is it just two? All those months spent barefoot and pregnant for two kids?"

"Al, this line of discussion is getting old. Really old."

"I'll tell you what, Juliet. I'll stop when you get yourself out of the kitchen and back here, where you belong."

"Thanks. And I miss you, too."

I could almost hear him blushing on the other end of the line. "Enough of this mushy stuff. Why are you calling? Who do you need me to run through NCIC now?"

"I'm trying to get some information about someone who does a lot of messing around on the Internet. I found out a bunch of stuff, but I'm no hacker, and I've kind of hit a brick wall. I was hoping you'd have some ideas for me."

Al paused, and it seemed to me that there was an uncomfortable silence.

"Al? You there? Got any ideas?"

"Yeah, I'm here. Okay, Juliet, can I trust you?"

"Sure. Of course you can trust me. You know that."

"I do have someone I've gone to a number of times for—let's call it specialized information. But if the boss lady found out I was using this guy, she'd hang me by my nuts."

"Nice image, Al. You've piqued my interest. Who's your expert?"

"I'm swearing you to secrecy, Juliet."

"I'm sworn, Al."

"Okay, remember Julio Rodriguez?"

A year or so before I'd quit, the office had represented Julio Rodriguez, a skinny kid from East L.A. who happened to be a computer genius. Using his cousin's ten-year-old Mac and an old acoustic modem, Julio managed to hack into the Immigration and Naturalization Service's files. It was months before anybody noticed that the number of green cards being issued to immigrants in Boyle Heights had shot through the roof. The papers had dubbed Julio the "Robin Hood of the Bario," and by the time the feds had tracked him down, he'd become a local folk hero. Marla Goldfarb herself had represented him and lost. Last I heard, Julio was serving a four-year sentence at FCI Lompoc.

"No kidding! Julio is out of jail? Is he some kind of expert witness or something?"

"No and yes," Al said.

"No and yes? What's that supposed to mean?"

"Yes, he's doing some, er, consulting, and no, he's not out of jail."

"Let me get this straight. Julio is still in jail?"

"At the Farm at Lompoc." The Farm is the minimum-security facility at Lompoc Federal Correction Institution. It's where white-collar criminals such as Michael Milkin and, apparently, Julio Rodriguez, serve their time.

"And you're using him as a consultant?"

"It's really not a big deal, Juliet. Sometimes, if I happen to have a question or two about a specific computer issue, and if I happen to be heading up to Lompoc anyway, I stop in to have a little conversation with Julio. And sometimes I give his mother a few bucks."

"How few?"

"A hundred dollars for every hour I spend with Julio."

I whistled. "Wow. Where the heck do you get that kind of money? You work for the federal defender, not for Johnny Cochran."

"I expense it. Over a couple of weeks. You see why Marla would lose her mind if she found out? I can't exactly submit this on a reimbursement form to the court, can I?"

All expert fees paid out by the federal defender's office have to be filed for approval with the federal district court. Marla, as a court officer, has the right to approve them herself, but ultimately the chief judge gets the paperwork.

Al was right. There was no way Marla would ever approve payments to Julio Rodriguez, a former client, even if he was the smartest cybergeek in all of California.

"So, Al, if I needed to have a chat with Julio, what would I do?"

"Are you still a member of the bar?"

"Of course I am."

"Then you would head up to Lompoc for a legal visit. If you tell Julio you used to work for us, he might not make you pay his mother in advance."

I considered for a moment whether I really wanted to be stuck behind the wheel of my car for the three hours it takes to get to Lompoc. Then I thought of Audrey.

"Thanks, Al. I'm going tomorrow."

"Tomorrow? Want some company?"

"What? You can go with me to Lompoc tomorrow? Are you serious?"

"I'm investigating a habeas case and I haven't been up to interview the client. He's at Lompoc."

"Al, I love you. I really do."

"We've got to get an early start. I'll pick you up at six."

"Jesus. That *is* early."

"You want to go or not?"

"Yes, yes. I want to go. Do you have my address?"

"Orange Drive, in Hancock Park, right?"

"Indeed."

"See you tomorrow."

"Okay. Thanks, Al."

"Thanks for what? We're just carpooling to Lompoc, right?"

"Right."

* * *

PETER wasn't thrilled when I told him he'd have to take the night off so I could wake up at the crack of dawn and head up to Lompoc, but he didn't freak out, either. He seemed sort of resigned to my investigation by that point.

The next morning I hauled myself out of bed before it was light and allowed myself a rare extra-large cup of coffee. One caffeine drink wouldn't kill the baby. Neither would two. Three was pushing it, but it was five-thirty in the morning, for crying out loud. I was waiting out on my front steps when Al pulled up in his monstrous Suburban.

"Nice to see you're taking that dependence on foreign oil thing to heart," I said as I scrambled up into the passenger seat, which seemed, to me at least, to be about eight feet off the ground.

"The United States has plenty of oil. We aren't dependent on anybody. That's all just lies spread by the government so we wouldn't figure out their real agenda in the Gulf War."

"And that was?"

"Illegally testing biological weapons on U.S. troops."

There was no way I was going to spend the next eight hours exploring the depths of Al's paranoid conspiracy theories.

"You're right, Al. Absolutely right. How could I have been so stupid? Can we change the subject now?"

"Fine. Live in ignorance. I don't care. Coffee?" He leaned over and picked up a thermos that was tucked under his seat.

"Mmm. Real coffee. I shouldn't. I had a cup or two this morning."

"Why shouldn't you?"

"Oh, you know, the baby and all."

"Oh, for Pete's sake. Elaine drank two pots of coffee a day when she was pregnant with our kids. And let's not even talk about the drinking and smoking."

"I know, I know. And you never put them in car seats, either, right?" I noticed, then, that Al had devised an intricate system of tucking his seat belt over his body and through his arm so that it appeared that he was wearing it while, in actuality, it hung, unbuckled and useless, at his side.

"Right," he said.

"Give me the thermos." I grabbed it, opened the top, and poured a few steaming inches into the little orange cup. Sipping the coffee, I grimaced at the weak, sour flavor. Obviously not a gourmet blend. But caffeine is caffeine, in whatever form it comes. I guzzled the last few mouthfuls in the cup and handed the thermos back to Al.

"Thanks," I said, and meant it.

We passed the rest of the drive in silence, listening to Al's favorite talk-radio host denounce the United Nations as a tool of the New World Order and claim to have personally witnessed black helicopters in formation over Roswell, New Mexico.

We pulled into Lompoc and headed over to the visiting building. We stopped at the reception desk, handed over our identification, and each filled out the form indicating that we were there for a legal visit. I glanced over at Al's form and noticed that he'd only written Julio's name.

"What about your habeas case, Al?" I asked.

"That? I decided not to bother with it today. I've got plenty of time before the petition is due."

"So you're just here for me?"

"Yup."

I smiled at him. What a guy.

We passed through the metal detectors, surrendering our cell phones to the guards, to be held until we left. I had a brief moment of panic, imagining something terrible happening to Ruby, and Peter unsuccessfully trying to reach me on my phone, but I pushed it out of my mind. Parents had survived thousands of years without cell phones. I could live without mine for a couple of hours.

Al and I walked up to the first door to the visiting room and stood, holding our passes up to the window and waiting, more or less patiently, for the guard manning the door to notice us. Despite the fact that I caught her eye through the reinforced window more than once, it took at least five minutes for the guard to buzz us in. By the time she had deigned to move her hand the two inches it took to reach the buzzer, I had begun, as always, to fume.

Prison guards can sometimes be the worst of the worst: petty, bureaucratic, wannabe cops who get off on asserting whatever power they can muster. Who in their right mind would want to spend his or her entire working day lording it over a bunch of pathetic, sometimes violent, losers whose fondest wish is usually to see you, if not dead, then beaten to a pulp? You have to really like the power dynamic to be willing to put up with the misery.

I can count on the fingers of one hand the number of times I've been treated with any kind of respect by a prison guard. They tend to view defense lawyers as one rung *below* their clients on the social scale. There's not a lot you can do about it, however. You just have to grit your teeth and do your best to ignore their games. So Al and I stood and waited for the rotund little guard in the too-tight uniform to buzz us through the steel-and-glass door. Then we walked through the hall and waited at the next locked door to get into the visiting room. It took us almost fifteen minutes to walk about twenty feet.

We made ourselves comfortable at one of the tables reserved for legal visits and waited some more, this time for Julio to be brought down to the visiting room. Visiting a client involves a whole lot of waiting. Just when I feared I was going to have to go out, visit the bathroom, and repeat the whole entrance rigmarole again, Julio was brought through a barred door into the room. One of the guards pointed him in our direction and he ambled over.

Julio was a good-looking kid, small and dark with decidedly Indian features. He wore his hair long and parted at the side like a curtain falling over his right eye. His face was broad and angled, with sharp cheekbones and a nose that was almost hooked. He looked like a Mayan statue—regal and just a little scary. He wore a pair of pressed jeans with a knife edge of a crease running precisely down the middle of his legs, a blue button-down shirt, and perfectly white Nikes—his prison uniform, but with a touch of class. He sat down gracefully and reached a small, strong hand with well-kept nails across the table.

"Al," he said, shaking his hand.

"Julio. Good to see you," Al replied.

"Ma'am." He extended a hand to me.

"Juliet Applebaum," I said, surprised at the softness of his palm, especially when contrasted with the firmness of his grasp.

"What can I do for you today?" Julio asked. In his voice I could hear the faintest trace of a Mexican accent.

"I was hoping you might be able to help me with a case I've been investigating," I said.

Al looked at me, eyebrows raised. I guess I'd never put it so bluntly before. The truth was unavoidable, however. I was investigating the murder of Abigail Hathaway, albeit unofficially.

"Has Al explained my terms to you?" Julio asked softly.

"One hundred dollars per hour, to be paid to your mother."

"Yes. I usually require some proof of prepayment, but if Al can vouch for you, I will allow you to pay after we speak."

"I can vouch for her," Al said.

"Fine," Julio replied.

"Okay, so here's the situation," I began.

It took about fifteen minutes for me to explain the entire history of Abigail Hathaway's death, her husband's affair, and the polyamorous computer club to Julio. He listened intently, never taking his eyes off mine. Initially it was disconcerting to have him staring at me so tenaciously, but I got used to it. I had never met anyone who sat as still and as quietly as Julio. Every once in a while he would nod at something I had said, or raise a quizzical eyebrow, asking, without words, for more information. Other than that, he was made of stone. Finally, when I had finished, he spoke.

"You should not have come here."

"What?" I was confused and not a little irritated. I mean, I'd driven three hours when I could barely manage to sit in one place for more than five minutes without my back seizing up, and this little creep was telling me I shouldn't have come? Wasn't my money good enough for him?

"You have wasted your time and money."

"And why would that be?" My voice came out stiffer and a little more prim than I would have liked.

"Because a computer-literate eight-year-old could have solved this problem for you."

"Well, Julio, here's the thing: I don't happen to know

any computer-literate eight-year-olds, and my two-and-a-half-year-old can barely manage to surf the Barbie website. So you're what I've got. Are you going to help me or not?"

"Yes. I will. But it is important for you to understand that this problem of yours is very easily solved."

"I understand."

"I am capable of much more demanding tasks."

"I understand."

"Despite that, you understand, my fee must apply."

"I understand."

"This is what you must do." Julio then described to me how I could access Daniel Mooney's account and trace his virtual steps. I have no idea if what he taught me was legal, but I decided not to worry about it. I took careful notes on Julio's instructions, not trusting my pregnancy-addled brain to remember anything. After he had finished, he asked for a sheet of paper and carefully wrote out a bill for one hour's work.

"Please deliver this to my mother with payment.

I took the bill and put it in my briefcase with the legal pad on which I'd made my copious notes. I reached out my hand to Julio who shook it once again.

"Good afternoon, Mrs. Applebaum," he said.

"Ms. But you can call me Juliet."

"Of course, Ms. Applebaum. It was a pleasure to assist you."

"Thank you, Julio. Is there anything we can help *you* with? Do you need anything?"

Julio smiled faintly. "Unless you have in your pocket a presidential pardon, I think that no, there is nothing you can do for me."

I smiled back at him. "Nope, fresh out of those. Sorry."

"Ah, well. Until next time, then."

"Hasta luego," Al interrupted, making no attempt at a Mexican accent whatsoever.

"Hasta proxima vez, Al," Julio said.

He rose and with a fluid, almost elegant stride, walked over to the guard, indicating that he was ready to go back up into the prison.

Al and I gathered our things and executed the elaborate door ballet in reverse, once again waiting much too long to be buzzed through.

"So, private eye Applebaum, did you get what you needed?" Al asked once we had settled ourselves into his car and driven through the gates of the prison.

"Yup. I think so. Now we'll just have to see if I can actually do this stuff on my computer."

"Julio's directions are usually pretty clear. Call me if you have any problems. Maybe my nine-year-old nephew can help you out."

"Ha, ha. Very funny, Al. Hey, listen, if I give you the hundred bucks, will you deliver it to Julio's mother?"

"Sure."

I wrote Al out a check, balancing my checkbook on my stomach.

"Hey, Juliet, interested in some barbecued oysters?"

Of course I was. We stopped at a little roadside shack and prepared to feast. I wasn't technically supposed to be eating oysters, but these were cooked, so I figured it was okay. Besides, there was no way I was going to sit and watch Al slurp up the contents of the oyster shells and lick sauce off his fingertips without having a plate of my own. I waited impatiently for my paper plate full of steaming shells drenched in spicy red sauce, and dove in headfirst when it arrived. As we gobbled our food, I brought Al up to date on my investigation. When I finished, he took a long draft of the one beer I had allowed

him to order, swallowed loudly, belched, and pointed a
thick finger at me.

"You, girl, have found your calling."

"What do you mean?"

"Investigation. Detection. Forget the courtroom crap.
Figuring out who done it. That's the fun part."

"You know, I always enjoyed that part of it. You're
right."

"You should hang out a shingle: "Juliet Applebaum,
Private Eye.""

"You're not the first person who's said that. Anyway,
stop worrying about my career and finish your food,
man! Let's get on the road."

We ate quickly, racing to see who could consume more
oysters. Al won. With a final belch, he pushed back his
chair and got up.

"Lunch is on you, Detective," he said.

I got home in plenty of time to hang out with Ruby and
Peter before dinner. We played a vigorous and cutthroat
game of Hungry Hippos, in the midst of which I noticed
that I was actually having a good time. While Ruby accu-
mulated every marble in the game, as she always did
through some innate power of control over plastic marble-
devouring hippopotamuses, I brought Peter up to speed
on what I had discovered. He seemed pretty impressed at
my detective skills, and even promised to help me surf
the Net for dirt on Daniel Mooney and Nina Tiger after
Ruby went to bed.

That night, Ruby seemed to sense that we wanted her
to get to bed so we could get to work on the computer.
First she needed an extra story. Then she needed another
drink of water. Then she peed in her overnight diaper and

couldn't stand the idea of sleeping in it. And so on. After
the third trip to the bathroom, I threatened her with no
candy the next day if she didn't go to sleep once and for
all. That got her. It's amazing how quickly kids discover
that candy is, in fact, the reason and purpose for human
existence.

Peter and I settled ourselves in front of the computer
and did our best to carry out Julio's instructions. Honestly, I have no idea what we did. While I love using my
computer, the technical details never remain in my brain
for very long. I always have the same experience as when
I took the bar exam. Walking in, the Rule Against Perpe-
tuities was as clear to me as the nose on the proctor's
face. As soon as I'd filled in my last circle and lay down
my number-two pencil, my brain flew open and promptly
flushed away that and every other arcane law that remains
on the books just to torment law students. They were
gone, as if they'd never even been there.

Somehow Peter and I managed to follow Julio's directions, and it didn't take long to accumulate a list of
aliases for both Daniel Mooney and Nina Tiger. We
started with Nina and spent a couple of hours tracing her
cyberfootsteps. I wasn't surprised to discover that Nina,
using different aliases, was an active member of a number of sex-based newsgroups. As "muffdvr" she explored
her lesbian sadomasochistic side. As "kittyhowl" she was
an expert on clitoral piercing. Most bizarrely, as "judys-
pal" she had a couple of hundred gay men convinced that
she was one of them. All pretty weird stuff, but nothing
particularly incriminating.

Finally, worried that spending too much time associat-
ing with the likes of Nina Tiger would kill our sex drives
once and for all, Peter and I decided to explore Daniel
Mooney's seamy side. Like Nina Tiger, he had his own

bunch of aliases—"mchoman," "boytoy2000," and even his own transvestite alias, "GRrrrL." The same kinky stuff as Nina, with the added twist that "GRrrrL" liked to pretend to be a pubescent girl and flirt with older men.

It didn't take long to find the piece of evidence that would put Daniel Mooney behind bars for the murder of his wife.

Fourteen

DANIEL Mooney's failing as a murderer was that he had the sophistication of a twelve-year-old. Using the alias "dollparts," and going no farther to cover his tracks, Abigail Hathaway's husband had posted the following advertisement on a website called "Soldiers of Fortune":

Wanted: Experienced soldier for special project. $5,000. Interested? Go to dollparts' private chat room on this site Monday nights, 2:00 A.M.

That was all, but it was everything. I immediately understood that Daniel Mooney had tried to hire someone to kill his wife. I hoped that Detective Carswell would understand the same. I'd been leaving him messages every couple of hours since two days before, when Audrey had come over to tell me about her suspicions about her stepfather, but Carswell still hadn't called me back. I called him again anyway. He wasn't at work. I spoke to the desk sergeant, asking him to find Carswell and let him know that it was a matter of great urgency that he call me, at any time, day or night. I could tell I wasn't being taken seriously and was pretty sure I wouldn't hear from Carswell that night.

Peter didn't go to work that night. Instead we crawled into bed together, both overcome with the enormity of what we had discovered. We lay side by side for a while, silently. Then, suddenly, I jumped.

"Oh, my God, Peter. Audrey. I don't know if she's still at her friend Alice's. What if she's home? What if she's all alone with him?"

"Abigail's daughter?"

"She could be in the house with him! What's to stop him from killing her, too?"

"She's probably at her friend's. That's where she told you she was going, right?"

"Yeah, but that was yesterday!"

"I'm sure she's still there. And, anyway, there's nothing we can do right now, Juliet. You called the detective."

"Maybe we should call nine-one-one. Or Social Services. Or something!" I was panicking.

"And tell them what? That we think her dad's a murderer because he was looking to chat with an experienced soldier on the web? No one would believe us. We need to talk to Detective Carswell."

"You're right. I know you're right. But what if something happens to her tonight and we could have prevented it? I couldn't live with myself. You didn't see her, Peter. She's so vulnerable."

"Look, he has no reason to suspect that she knows anything. And anyway, he'd have to be a total moron to hurt her now, so soon after her mother's death. That would immediately draw attention to him. He won't do it. It wouldn't make any sense."

"No, it wouldn't. We'll just have to hope that he acts sensibly."

Peter and I slept little that night. Finally, at about 6:00 A.M., I couldn't wait any longer. I picked up the phone and dialed the Santa Monica P.D. Miraculously, Detective Carswell was in.

To my surprise, he didn't dismiss me right away. On the contrary, he took me much more seriously than I had expected and every bit as seriously as I hoped. Within half an hour he was on my doorstep, accompanied by another detective, a younger man who sported the same military haircut but wore, instead of a suit, a pair of khakis and a blue blazer. Kind of like an oversized Catholic schoolboy.

I showed the two into my kitchen and offered them coffee. They accepted.

"Ms. Applebaum, please tell us what you've discovered," Carswell said, not patronizing me in the slightest. Finally.

I described my computer investigation. Carswell seemed impressed at my savvy.

"You figured out how to track his steps through all his various aliases?" he asked

I certainly wasn't going to tell him about Julio.

"It's really very easy," I replied. "Any computer-literate eight-year-old could do it."

"Still, I'm impressed," he said, not quite grudgingly.

I smiled, feeling like I'd earned a gold star from my kindergarten teacher.

"We'd like to see the files you've downloaded," the other officer said.

I showed them into my office and to my computer. The

ad, which I had not only copied into my hard drive but also bookmarked, was on the screen. The young detective sat down at my chair, pulled a couple of floppy disks out of his coat pocket, and proceeded to make copies not only of the ad but also of the many conversations of the polyamorous newsgroup. Then the two sat with me for another hour, taking notes, while I described in detail all my investigations of the past week. I left out Audrey's visit to me, because I'd promised her that I wouldn't tell them about her, and my meeting with Julio, because I didn't want Al to get into trouble.

I actually intended to tell Carswell about how Nina Tiger had found me going through her mailbox, but I couldn't bring myself to do it. It was, after all, a crime, and I hope I can be forgiven for failing to confess it to a police officer. Detective Carswell didn't *need* to know that I'd broken into her mailbox or that I'd had a confrontation with her. It wouldn't help or hurt his case any. I was rationalizing and I knew it, but I couldn't help myself.

Detective Carswell and his partner made me go over everything a second time and then rose to leave.

"Wait!" I said. "What are you going to do now?"

The two cops glanced at each other. "We'll review this information and have our computer experts track Mooney's Internet activities," Carswell said.

"And then?"

"Well, if it all checks out, if we're convinced from the evidence that this was murder and not a hit-and-run accident, and if we can convince the judge that the evidence against him amounts to probable cause, then we'll get a warrant and arrest Daniel Mooney."

I couldn't resist. "Pretty relevant information, after all, don't you think?"

Carswell looked at me for a moment. Then, miraculously, his stony face cracked into a smile. "Pretty relevant after all," he agreed.

"Ms. Applebaum, it's very important that you tell no one of the things you have discovered. We don't want to take the chance that word will get to the suspect before we're absolutely ready to act on this information," he continued.

"Right. Of course. I was a public defender. I know how it works."

At that piece of information Carswell's partner looked really worried.

"Ms. Applebaum, your defense prejudice isn't going to influence you, is it?" the young officer asked.

This steamed me. "Look, I just spent who knows how much time and energy trying to prove that this guy killed his wife! Why would I blow it now?"

Somewhat mollified, the two detectives left our house.

Fifteen

THE next morning, Ruby woke me up earlier than normal. I plopped her in front of *Sesame Street* and headed out to the curb to get the newspaper. Cursing the delivery boy who had once again tossed the paper directly onto one of our sprinkler heads, I threaded my way, barefoot, over the grass. I picked up the soggy paper by one corner and went back inside. I tossed the paper into the oven and turned it on to about 200 degrees. I figured that as long as I stayed well below the famous Fahrenheit 451, nothing would burst into flames. I made myself a cup of tea, microwaved a few pancakes for Ruby, and settled down at the kitchen counter. Hoping that the paper was dry, I reached in with an oven mitt, grabbed it by a corner, and pulled it out. And then I started shouting.

"Peter! Peter!"

My husband came tearing out of the bedroom, stark naked.

"The baby? Is it the baby?"

I shoved the paper into his hands. He screamed and dropped it.

"Ouch! That's hot!" he howled.

"Oh. Sorry. Look! Look at the front page!"

He leaned over the floor and read aloud, "Nursery School Teacher's Husband Arrested for Murder!"

"They arrested him!"

"I can see that."

Carswell wouldn't give me any more information when I called him, so whatever I know I learned from that front-page article in the *Los Angeles Times*. Abigail Hathaway's own car matched the description of the one that had run her down; she drove a two-year-old Mercedes sedan, black. Her car wasn't at home, and when asked about it, Daniel Mooney apparently claimed to have assumed it was at the school. He said he hadn't bothered to look for it after she'd been killed. But it wasn't in the nursery school parking lot. The police searched the city, but unsurprisingly, it was nowhere to be found. The newspaper speculated that if the car had been abandoned after the murder, particularly if the keys had been left in the ignition, one or another of Los Angeles's hyperefficient car theft rings would have had it lifted, painted, and on its way to Mexico or China within a couple of hours.

So there it was: Abigail was murdered by her own husband, driving her own car.

Peter and I read the newspaper article together, sitting side by side at the kitchen table. Reading about the crime, I felt this weird combination of sadness for Abigail and her poor daughter, and satisfaction at a job well done. It was sort of like what I'd felt after winning a trial. I'd be feeling on top of the world, proud of my success, and flying high on my ego. Then I'd look over to the family of the victim, or the victim himself, and feel a little deflated.

Sure, my client had gotten off because I'd done such a good job of convincing the jury of his lack of guilt or of the victim's complicity. But criminal law isn't a computer game. It isn't just a question of winning or losing and racking up points. My victory meant that someone else lost. When that someone was just the government—if, for example it was a drug case and nobody except the DEA cared if my client was convicted—then it was easy to revel in my success. But often enough, my clients had actually hurt someone. It was a heck of a lot harder to find myself happy about winning their freedom under those circumstances.

I felt a similar bittersweetness that morning. Yes, I succeeded. I'd found Abigail's murderer. But while Audrey was surely a lot safer with her stepfather behind bars, she was still an orphan, now more than ever.

"Maybe I should give Audrey a call," I said. "She's probably at her friend Alice's house."

"That's not a bad idea," Peter answered.

I reached for the phone, but before I even dialed, it rang. "Hello?"

"Juliet! This is Audrey! Isn't this awesome! Isn't this just totally bitchin' what happened to Danny? That nimrod's in jail! He is *in jail*!" Audrey was positively giddy.

"Yes, I guess it's awesome. But how are you doing? You must be pretty freaked out by this all." I looked over at Peter and mouthed silently, "Audrey." He nodded.

"Freaked out? No way! I'm happier than I've ever been in my whole life! He is G-O-N-E gone! Out of my life forever!" she shouted.

"So what are you going to do now?" I asked her.

"My aunt's flying in tonight, so I guess I'll just stay at home with her. I've gotta decide about New Jersey. What do you think I should do?"

I thought for a moment. "I guess I think you should go. New Jersey's not so bad. It's close to New York!"

"Hey! I didn't think of that. New York. Now, *that* would be bitchin'."

I laughed. "I guess it would. It sure can be. Promise me you'll keep in touch, okay?"

"Definitely! What's your E-mail address? I'll E-mail you!"

What would the world be like without the Internet? I wonder. How did we ever survive, a mere five years ago, before everyone had her very own E-mail account?

I gave Audrey my E-mail address, and she promised to write. I hung up the phone.

"She's staying with her friend until her aunt comes," I said.

"How did she sound?"

"Relieved. Happy really," I said. "I'm just glad she's safe."

The phone rang again. It was Stacy.

"Can you believe this?" she positively shrieked.

"Yes, actually because—"

"And you thought it was Bruce LeCrone! Ha. Please!"

"Well, actually, I was the one who—"

"Like Bruce would do that. Really. But her husband! I always knew that there was something fishy about—"

"Stacy! If you'd just shut up for a moment, I'll tell you how I solved this murder!"

That shut her up. I described the events of the past week or so to Stacy, lingering over details of my derring-do. Once again I kept Julio out of it, as I'd promised Al, but no other element of the story was spared my dramatization. By the end of my tale I'd actually managed to leave Stacy speechless. I think that's the first time that anyone has ever accomplished that. My story complete, I

said good-bye, hung up the phone and looked compla-
cently over at Peter.

"Uh, Juliet, didn't Detective Carswell ask you not to
reveal any details of the investigation?" he said.

I blanched. "I totally forgot. Do you think it's okay?
Do you think Stacy will tell anyone?"

He looked at me.

I answered my own question. "Of course she will. Oh,
no no no no."

I immediately dialed her number, but got voice mail.
She had already begun to broadcast. I left a frantic message, begging her not to tell a soul. She was definitely
going to ignore it, but it was the best I could do. I put my
head down on the kitchen counter and moaned. "I had to
tell the single biggest gossip in Los Angeles. I hope this
doesn't get back to Carswell."

"Don't worry, sweetie," Peter said, patting my head.
"Stacy and the detective don't exactly travel in the same
circles. It'll probably be fine."

I didn't make the same mistake again. Both Al and
Jerome called me that morning, and I remained discreet,
expressing only my happiness that Daniel Mooney had
been apprehended and nothing else. I didn't let my guard
down until I heard from Lilly Green.

Lilly called me from her car phone.

"Juliet! I just got my nails done and I'm right around
the corner from you. Meet me for a cup of coffee at the
Living Room and tell me everything about your murder!"

I threw a baseball cap on over my hair, quickly
dragged on a pair of leggings and one of Peter's flannel
shirts, and promising Ruby and Peter that I would not be
gone long, rushed out the door. As I was tearing up the
block on my way to meet Lilly at the homey little café
she favored, it occurred to me to wonder if I would have

dropped everything so quickly for a friend who wasn't a famous, Oscar-winning movie star. Just how starstruck was I? I couldn't answer the question and decided not to bother trying. I liked Lilly, and if I also liked being seen with her, well, that didn't make me any worse or any better than the rest of Los Angeles. In L.A., being starstruck is one's civic duty.

By the time I got to the café, huffing and puffing and beet-red with the exertion of my block-and-a-half walk, Lilly was already there, lounging on an overstuffed sofa, sipping a latté out of a cup the size of a basketball. She wore a pair of jeans and an old, ratty turtleneck sweater. Her hair was casually wound around her head and held in place with a chopstick. She looked gorgeous. I sighed for a moment, imagining just how beautiful I looked right then, exploding out of Peter's old shirt, my leggings fraying at the seams with the effort of containing the bulk of my thighs. Silently repeating my mantra "I'm not fat, I'm pregnant," I gave Lilly a hug and sank down next to her on the couch.

"Nonfat latte," I said to the rail-thin young thing who had instantly appeared to take my order. I got service like that only when I was with Lilly. Alone, I'd have been waiting for hours.

"Decaf?" she asked, except it sounded like "detaf" because she was having difficulty talking through the large silver stud embedded in her tongue.

"No. Caf-caf," I said.

The waitress looked disapprovingly at my belly and turned away.

"Lilly, can I bum a cigarette? Or a line of cocaine?" I asked, loud enough for the waitress to hear. Her back stiffened and she hustled off. "Why is it everyone thinks they can tell a pregnant woman what to drink, eat, whatever? I mean, for crying out loud, it's only coffee. Women in France drink coffee and swill red wine the whole time they're pregnant. No one bugs *them*."

"Yes, but then they give birth to little Frenchmen."

"Good point."

"So, you were right about Abigail Hathaway's husband!" Lilly said, getting to the point.

Once again conveniently forgetting my promise not to discuss the case with anyone, I filled Lilly in on my role in the arrest of Daniel Mooney.

"Herma Wang should have her license revoked," Lilly said once I'd finished.

"Why?"

"For not figuring out that he was so violent, that's why. She was perfectly willing to tell me that the family is in crisis and go on and on about all the suppressed rage, but did she put two and two together and realize someone was actually in danger? God forbid."

"She told you that? What is she, the Liz Smith of shrinks? Confidentiality be damned—I know a movie star!"

"I know. Ridiculous, isn't it? I can only imagine what she's told people about *us*." Lilly grimaced. "I'm doing my best just not to think about it."

"She wouldn't talk *about* you. She just likes talking *to* you. She's telling you stuff so you'll keep having lunch with her and she can tell people she's friends with a movie star. It's hardly unusual. I mean, look at me, running out of my house at a moment's notice to meet you for coffee."

Lilly laughed uncomfortably, not sure if I was kidding.

At that moment my coffee showed up. I slurped at it loudly, for the pierced waitress's benefit.

"Anyway, what else did Wang tell you?" I asked.

"Oh, not much more than that. The family was having terrible problems. They were considering divorce. The daughter was acting out, having problems in school, hanging with a fast crowd. That kind of thing."

"Audrey, she's the daughter, is kind of a lost soul," I said. "She has this horrible shaved and dyed hairdo that I'm sure she got just to torture her mother."

"They did a lot of torturing of each other, according to Herma," Lilly said. "Not a very easy relationship. Abigail had high expectations, and Audrey had a hard time fulfilling them, or something like that. Apparently Mooney and the girl didn't like each other, and that was a source of real tension in the marriage."

"High expectations? Sounds like every mother-daughter relationship I've ever heard of," I said.

"Not mine." Lilly sounded bitter. "My mother expected me to get pregnant at fifteen and spend my life living in a trailer park with six kids by six different men. She's sorely disappointed that I've exceeded her expectations."

"God, are our kids going to be sitting here in thirty years having this discussion about us?" I asked, imagining Ruby and the twins bemoaning our various flaws over latte or proton shakes or whatever they'll be drinking then.

"God forbid." Lilly shuddered. "Why didn't he just leave her? Why *kill* her?" she asked.

"Money. It must have been about money. She owned everything they had as her separate property. It's likely that he would have had to walk away from the marriage empty-handed."

"But I imagine that he must have hated her, too. Don't you think he would have had to, to murder her?"

"I wonder."

"It's always someone in the family, isn't it?"

"What do you mean?"

"It's always a family member who's the murderer."

"Usually. Or, if not family, then certainly someone the victim knew. Stranger-on-stranger crimes are much rarer."

"But that's what we're all afraid of. Isn't that ironic? We're so afraid of being killed by some serial killer but it's our loved ones we really should be afraid of."

I looked at Lilly for a minute, wondering what was inspiring these morbid thoughts. "Lilly, are you trying to tell me something? Have you murdered someone?"

She laughed. "Actually, you know what? There are only two people I can even imagining killing. Guess who?"

"Your agent?"

"No. Although that's an idea."

"The director of your last picture."

"Ouch. That stings."

"Sorry. So who?"

"Well, one is my ex-husband, obviously. The other is my mother." Lilly laughed grimly. "And instead of killing either of them I bought them each a house."

"You bought Archer a house?" I almost shouted.

"Community property bought Archer a house. And a boat. And two cars. And a share in Planet Hollywood and so on and so on and so on."

"Wow. You know what, Lilly? maybe we should get married. I could use some extra cash."

"Very funny. Ha, ha, ha."

Suddenly I had a thought. "Hey, Lilly, are the twins still in preschool?"

"Yes. Next year they'll start kindergarten at Cross-roads," she said proudly.

It occurred to me that I didn't even know where Amber and Jade went to school. "Where do they go now?"

"Temple Beth El," she said.

That stopped me in my tracks. Lilly Green, the person-ification of blond, Aryan womanhood, sent her kids to a Jewish school? She noticed my bemused expression.

"Archer's mother is Jewish," she explained. "And the girls didn't get in anywhere else. We applied pre-Oscar."

"Oh. Do you like it?"

"I love it. I love that the girls walk around the house singing "*Shabet shalom,* hey!" she warbled.

"*Sha*-bat."

"Right, right. *Shabat shalom,* hey! I have a terrific idea! Why don't I ask the principal if they still have slots available for next year?"

"No. No. That's okay." It probably sounds crazy, but Peter and I had never discussed the religion thing. We celebrated whatever holiday came around and just sort of assumed that things would work themselves out. I couldn't see asking him to send Ruby to a Jewish pre-school. That would be like taking sides.

"Really, I don't mind. I'll ask her when I pick up the girls tomorrow."

"You'd better not. You know, the whole Jewish thing."

"Oh, don't be ridiculous. There are plenty of *goys* like me at the school. I'm going to ask her. It can't hurt."

We talked for a while longer about Daniel Mooney and about whether he'd plead guilty or go to trial. After we'd finished our coffees, Lilly offered me a ride home.

"No, I think I'll walk. I need the exercise."

It was only after she'd gone that I realized she'd left me with the check. Again.

sixteen

OVER the next few weeks the newspapers were full of the tragedy of Abigail Hathaway and Daniel Mooney. The case was taken away from the Santa Monica D.A. and moved to downtown Los Angeles. Mooney was charged with first-degree murder, which carries the death penalty, and thus no possibility of bail. Audrey called a few more times, but we never got together. She told me that she had decided to finish out the school year before moving to New Jersey and was living in her house with her aunt. She seemed to have gotten over her first blush of giddiness at her stepfather's arrest, and expressed her eagerness to put the whole ugly business behind her. I agreed that that was probably a good idea, but secretly wondered if she ever would be able to put the loss of her mother behind her. Could anyone?

My pregnancy proceeded and I closed in on the final month, looking forward with mounting impatience to Isaac's arrival. I tried to spend as much time as possible with Ruby, preparing her as best I could for the upheaval the new baby would cause in all our lives.

One night, after putting Ruby to sleep and sending Peter off to work, I lay in bed, trying to fall asleep. I tossed and turned, or rather, I tried to toss but couldn't quite manage to heft my belly from one side of the bed to another. Finally, frustrated and hungry, I got up and made myself a peanut-butter-and-jelly sandwich. Recalling Peter's recent irritation at me for getting crumbs in the bed, I decided to eat in my office, and play on the computer for a while. I logged on, licked my fingers clean, and checked out what was happening on *Moms Online*. I lurked for a while in a chat room, but couldn't manage to work up any interest in the sore-nipple discussion.

I decided to check out how Nina Tiger was dealing with the arrest of her lover. I clicked over to Dejanews and plugged in her name. I soon tired of reading her vitriolic defenses of Mooney's innocence but, unfortunately, I wasn't tired enough to go to sleep. Bored, I typed in Daniel Mooney's screen names. As I had already read in tigress's correspondence, Coyote was the topic of much conversation among the polyamorous. Nobody had seemed to notice mchoman's absence from the newsgroup in which Mooney had participated using that alias, but boytoy2000 had been sorely missed by the more raunchy of his cyberpals. Because none of his buddies had linked him to Daniel Mooney, there was much speculation about where boytoy2000 had gone.

I input the last of Mooney's aliases, GRrrrL. That's when I got the shock of my life. GRrrrL, Mooney's female alter ego, had posted as recently as last night. Shaken, I called out for Peter. He came tearing into my office.

"Is it happening? Are you in labor?" he asked, almost hysterically.

"No. Look." I held a trembling finger out to the screen.

"Juliet! You have *got* to stop doing that to me. Look at what?"

"Dejanews has postings from GRrrrL, Daniel Mooney's alias, from last night."

Peter quickly scrolled down the screen.

"This is what our tax dollars are going for? Web access in prisons?" he asked, outraged.

"There is no Web access in the county jail. GRrrrL is posting from outside."

"Then there's got to be a mistake. Mooney's in jail. Dejanews must be wrong."

"They're not wrong. GRrrrL is posting."

Peter and I sat staring at the screen for a moment.

"I'm going to find GRrrrL," I said.

"How?"

"Watch."

I scrolled up and found the address of the newsgroup on which GRrrrL's most recent post had appeared. I clicked the "new message" box and posted the following message under the subject heading "GRrrrL sought":

GRrrrL—I want to talk to you. E-mail me and set up private chat.

"Why not just E-mail GRrrrL directly?" Peter asked.

"Because I want whoever's using the account to know just where I tracked GRrrrL down."

"Oh. Now what?" Peter asked.

"Now we wait," I said grimly.

We waited. We waited for two hours and heard nothing. Finally, exhausted and drained, we set the computer to download E-mail every half hour and went to bed. The next morning I leaped out of bed and rushed to the computer. At 6:30 A.M. I had received a message from GRrrrL. Fingers shaking, I opened it.

Private chat at 4:00 P.M. See you there!

The rest of the day passed in something of a blur. Ruby, sensing that I was preoccupied and tense, matched me mood for mood. When she wasn't whining she was throwing a tantrum or stomping around the house in a huff. Peter and I spent the day frantically trying to entertain her, but she had the attention span of a flea. No game was good enough, no toy fun enough. Finally, in desperation, Peter took her to our old standby, the Santa Monica Pier. We figured he'd tire her out on the carousel and rides. While they were gone I mostly paced around the house. Oprah distracted me for a few minutes but not long. Finally, at ten minutes to four, I heard Peter's car pull in the driveway.

I rushed to the front door and opened it in time for him to tiptoe in, carrying a sleeping Ruby in his arms. Walking as quietly as possible, he took her into her room, put her in her crib, and closed the door.

"Let's go," he said.

We went into my office, closed the door, logged on, and entered the chat room.

GRrrrl? Are you here?
Here I am. I know who you are.

I looked up at Peter, scared. "How does he know me?"

"I don't know. Is your tag line somewhere on your message?"

"No, just my e-mail address."

How do you know who I am? I wrote back.
Never mind. What do you want?

I paused for a moment. What did I want? To know who he was, I suppose.

Who are YOU? I typed.
GRrrrL.
No, who are you IRL?

"IRL?" Peter asked, reading over my shoulder.
"In real life."

Who do you think I am? GRrrrL asked me back.
This screen name belongs to Daniel Mooney.
Then I'm Daniel Mooney.
Daniel Mooney is in the county jail. He can't log on.
Poor Daniel. Locked in jail.

I looked up at Peter again. "What's going on here?" I asked.

He shook his head. "Juliet, what if GRrrrL placed the ad for the hired killer? What if Daniel Mooney didn't do it?"

The thought had crossed my mind at the same time. After all, the only hard evidence against Mooney was the ad. The rest was purely circumstantial. I decided to give it a shot.

Do you know who killed Abigail? I typed.
Daniel Mooney killed Abigail.
Is that true? Do you know that for a fact?
Do YOU know that for a fact? GRrrrL asked back.

Now GRrrrL was messing with me.
"Peter, maybe I should just ask him straight out."

"Go for it." He squeezed my shoulder and kissed my cheek. I took a deep breath and then started typing.

Did YOU kill Abigail?

There was a pause. Finally GRrrrL replied,

Did YOU?
No, I did not. You didn't answer my question. DID YOU KILL ABIGAIL HATHAWAY?
Bye-bye, Juliet.

And GRrrrL was gone. Peter and I sat, staring at the computer screen for a moment. I copied the text of our conversation into a file on my computer and sent it to print. As I clicked the print button, I had an epiphany.

"I know who that was."

"You do?" Peter asked doubtfully.

"Nina Tiger."

"His lover?"

"It's got to be her. Think about it. They have the same access provider. All she'd have to do would be to log on as a guest and input the password he uses for that alias. Who else would know his password? It has to be her."

"You don't know my password. Why would she know his?" Peter said.

"Gee, I don't know. Could it be, perhaps, Cthulhu?"

"Hey!" he shouted. "How did you know that?"

"Oh, please, Mr. Owns a First Edition of Every Book H. P. Lovecraft Ever Wrote."

"I can't believe you."

"Could we get back to the issue at hand?"

"I can't *believe* you."

"Peter!"

"Okay, okay. How would Nina Tiger have known who you are?"

"She must have compared notes with Mooney. I introduced myself to him, and he probably told her about me. How many pregnant women with red hair could have been following them around? She put two and two together and came up with me."

"Juliet?"

"What?"

"What are you talking about?"

Then I remembered that I hadn't mentioned my run-in with tigress. With a huge amount of trepidation, I told him about it. To Peter's credit, he managed to suppress whatever anger I knew he must have felt. He looked at me horrified and then seemed to make a decision not to discuss it.

"Okay, so it's Nina Tiger. So what?" he said.

I thought. True, so what? So what if she was logging on as her imprisoned lover? It was weird, but it didn't mean anything. Then I realized something.

"She never answered my question."

"What?"

"She never said she didn't kill Abigail."

Seventeen

I called Detective Carswell and left another of my famous messages for him. This time I asked for and received his fax number and faxed over a copy of my chat with GRrrrL. That would make him call back.

"Peter?" I said.

"What?"

"If tigress killed Abigail, that means that Daniel Mooney didn't."

"Unless they were in it together."

"Either way, the murderer is still out there, and so is Audrey." I began to pace nervously. "I wish that detective would call me back."

"Juliet, there's no reason to think that Audrey is in any danger. Tigress hasn't done anything to her yet. Why would she start now?"

"I suppose. God, I wish Carswell would call me."

I called the station house again, telling the woman who took my call that it was an emergency. Something about

the tone of my voice must have convinced her how serious I was. She put me on hold. Within a couple of minutes I was talking to Detective Carswell.

I apprised the detective of my online conversation with
GRrrrL and explained why I thought that Nina Tiger was
the only person who could have had access to Daniel
Mooney's alias and password. Sounding somewhat dubi-
ous, he asked to explain how I'd tracked GRrrrL down.
After a couple of frustrating minutes trying to explain
Dejanews to a man who just barely understood the con-
cept of E-mail, I asked him to please come over so I could
show him what I was talking about. He agreed. He and his
young sidekick showed up at our door half an hour later.

I led the police officers directly to my computer, and I
logged on and showed them what I'd found.

The young cop looked at Carswell. "Maybe we should
talk to Ms. Tiger," he said.

"We'd planned on interviewing her anyway. She's on
the witness list," Carswell said, nodding his head.

The younger officer borrowed my phone and called the
station house. Eavesdropping, I heard him ask for a DMV
address on Nina Tiger.

"Is that all you have?" he said into the receiver.

He covered the receiver with his hand and spoke to
Carswell. "Last known address is in Santa Barbara."

"She lives here, in Venice," I interrupted. "Remember,
I told you that I followed her?"

He turned back to the phone. "Check for a Venice
address." He waited a moment and then replied, "Okay,
we'll get it from the witness."

"What's going on?" Carswell asked.

"No Venice address listed."

"Ms. Applebaum," Carswell asked me, "do you
remember the address of her apartment in Venice?"

"It was on Rose Street," I said. "A fourplex."

"The house number?" he asked.

I racked my brain. "I'm sorry. I don't remember. It was in the middle of the block. Mediterranean. Kind of like all the others on that block."

"Would you know it if you saw it?"

"I think so. And I'd definitely recognize her car."

I drove with the detectives in their unmarked car, an anonymous blue, late-model American sedan, to Venice. Peter had been loath to let me go, but I had insisted. We drove onto the block, and I directed Carswell and the young detective to Nina Tiger's apartment building. I pointed out the Mustang convertible parked at the curb.

"That's her car," I said.

"Now, you wait right here, Ms. Applebaum," the young detective said.

"Don't move," Carswell reiterated.

I promised not to, and settled more comfortably in the backseat of the car, propping my feet up. I watched them head off up the path and imagined tigress's face when she opened the door to them.

I hadn't gotten very far in my fantasy when I noticed the door to the building open. With a flash of red hair and long legs, Nina Tiger strode down the path toward her car. They must have missed her!

For a moment I puzzled over what to do. I was under strict orders not to move. On the other hand, no way was I going to let her get away. She might have been on her way to Audrey's house! I wrenched the car door open, leaned my head out, and shouted.

"YO! Tigress!"

She stopped dead in her tracks and looked around her,

finally spotting me. Meanwhile, I was having problems getting myself out of the car. I gave a final heave and staggered out onto the sidewalk. She looked at me blankly for a minute, and then I could see a flash of recognition cross her face.

"My mailbox!" she said, and ran over to me, hands on her hips. "Who are you? Why are you calling me 'tigress'? Are you on one of my lists? What's your name?"

With the final question she reached me and, sticking a finger out, poked me in the chest. Hard.

"Hey! Watch it!" I said, batting away her hand.

"No! *You* watch it." She pushed me. I staggered back and swayed, scrambling with my feet to keep from falling. At that moment I heard a voice shout, "Police, put your hands up!"

"What the hell?" tigress said, turning around and spotting the detectives running from the house. "Are you out of your goddamn minds?" she screeched. "This bitch is assaulting me!"

"I am not!" I said indignantly. "She pushed me!"

"She broke into my mailbox!"

"Well, yeah, but not today!"

By then the detectives had reached us. Carswell grabbed tigress by the arm and dragged her away from me. The young guy helped me steady myself.

"Are you okay, Ms. Applebaum?" he asked.

"You know her? What's going on here? Is she a cop?" Nina yelled.

Carswell led her a few feet away and asked calmly, "Are you Nina Tiger?"

"Yeah. So what? Am I under arrest?"

"I have some questions for you, Miss Tiger. Shall we continue this inside?"

"No way you are coming into my apartment!" she said with a snarl.

"Shall we continue this at the station house?"

She shrugged off his hand, angrily. "Look, if this is about Abigail Hathaway, I had nothing to do with that. I was in Santa Barbara, at my mother's house. Three of her bridge partners saw me there. You can call them all!"

Detective Carswell paused for a minute and then said, "We simply have a number of questions for you. Nothing serious. Why don't we go upstairs and discuss it."

"Fine." She stormed up the path to her front door.

Carswell looked at the younger detective and said, "Take Ms. Applebaum home and then come get me. ASAP." He followed tigress into the house.

THE detective dropped me off at home, and I walked in, shouting out, "I'm home!"

"How'd it go?" asked Peter.

"She has an alibi."

"Oh. Sorry."

"She could have hired someone to kill Abigail," I said, grasping at straws.

"I guess so. The police will figure it out," Peter said.

"Yeah, I suppose they will. Is Ruby still asleep?"

"I guess so."

"You guess so? It's late. We'd better wake her up."

I walked into Ruby's room and gently shook her awake. She responded by squawking in outrage and promptly bursting into tears. I tried pulling out her Tickle-Me-Elmo. The screaming continued. I grabbed her Madeleine doll. No effect. Finally, desperate, I said, "Hey, Peanut, want to go visit the Barbie website?"

"No. I hate Barbie."

"You do not, Ruby. You have twenty Barbies. You *love* Barbie. Let's go visit the website. It'll be fun, I promise."

I plopped Ruby on the chair at my desk and logged on. I quickly found the Barbie website, and set Ruby up selecting the accessory set for her personalized "Friend of Barbie" doll.

I leaned against my desk, too tired to stand but too lazy to get another chair. Ruby looked so sweet, her curls tumbling into her eyes, her face screwed up with concentration. I wondered, for the thousandth time, how she was going to tolerate another baby in the house. This child was so used to being the center of attention, the queen of the castle. The birth of a prince was going to be quite a shock.

Ruby interrupted my reverie. "Mommy, the computer said 'You've got mail.' "

"Oh, that means an E-mail came in. Want to help me get it?"

"Yeah!"

"Move the mouse over to the little mailbox symbol."

She followed my instructions.

"Now click twice."

She did.

It was a piece of junk E-mail—spam. I showed Ruby how to delete it and then helped her click back over to Barbie. And then, watching her dress Barbie in a fuchsia boa and purple pedal pushers, I figured it out. I figured out who GRrrrL was.

Eighteen

I'M not sure why I did what I did next. In hindsight, it was definitely an idiotic move. But, at the time, I really didn't think I was putting myself in harm's way. I felt pretty confident that I was right, but I knew that after the tigress fiasco the Santa Monica Police Department wasn't going to accompany me on any more detective expeditions. I certainly wasn't going to ask Peter to come with me, as that would have meant bringing Ruby along, too. So I told my husband that I had to go out, making up an excuse about going to the drugstore to buy pads for when I came home from the hospital. He was only too glad to watch the baby, relieved that I hadn't sent him off to buy feminine hygiene products.

I drove across town on the freeway and up the Pacific Coast Highway to Santa Monica Canyon. I was going very fast, and it's a miracle I wasn't pulled over for speeding. Still, it felt like hours before I finally pulled up in front of Abigail Hathaway's Tudor house. I rammed the car into park and, slamming the door behind me, ran up the path. I rang the bell and, too impatient to wait, pounded on the door.

After a moment or two, Audrey opened it. She looked the same as always, except she'd had half her hair shaved off again and the rest redyed a sapphire blue. She sported a new stud in her nose, a stone that matched her hair. She smiled nervously when she saw me. "Hi, Juliet! What's going on? You look . . ." She didn't finish the sentence.

I looked at my reflection in the long, narrow window next to the front door. I was wearing my usual uniform of leggings and shirt, but a length of thigh was peeping out a torn seam. I hadn't even noticed. My hair was dragged off my face with a rubber band, and I wore not the slightest trace of makeup.

"Are you okay?" Audrey asked me.

"We need to talk. Is your aunt home?"

"No, she just left for the grocery store. Talk about what?" She held the door halfway closed.

"Let me in, Audrey." I pushed against the door.

She held it against my hand.

"What's going on, Juliet? You looked freaked."

"Let me in *now*." I jerked the door open and pushed by her.

"Fine, come in. What's up with you?" she asked. She sounded angry but also a little nervous.

"I know about GRrrrL, Audrey," I said, standing in the hall.

"Who? What girl?"

"Don't lie to me, Audrey. I know that you're using your stepfather's computer and that your screen name is GRrrrL."

"It is *not* his computer. My mom bought it. It's a family computer. I'm perfectly entitled to use it. And anyway, I'm not even using that computer. I'm using my mom's laptop. One of the stupid teachers from her stupid school dropped it off a couple of days ago."

She stalked off into the living room and shut the door after herself. I hustled in behind her and opened it to find her bent over her mother's desk. She slammed shut a drawer as I walked in. Tossing her half-bald head, Audrey walked over to the couch and sat down. She held her chin high and crossed her legs primly. I could see the pulse beating in her throat.

"So you figured out my screen name. So what? What does that make you, some kind of genius? I, like, basically told you it was me."

I sat down next to her. She still looked so vulnerable to me, so young despite her pathetic attempts at "cool."

"Audrey, have you told the police about your screen name?" I asked her.

She looked at me incredulously. "No. Why should I? It's none of their business." She started picking at a cuticle on her right thumbnail. A bead of bright-red blood appeared. She stuck her finger in her mouth and sucked on it, like a baby.

"Audrey, it is their business. You know that." Was she really as obtuse as she was pretending to be? "Listen to me. You have to tell the police, because you can be sure Daniel will."

"Oh, please, like they could care less about my screen name."

"Audrey, the police confiscated Daniel's computer, didn't they?"

"Yeah, that's why I had to wait like a week to get online. I couldn't do anything until Maggie suddenly remembered that she'd borrowed my mom's computer and brought it back to me. I'm surprised the bitch didn't just keep it."

I started to defend the nursery school teacher but then shook my head. I wasn't going to let Audrey distract me. I got back to the point. "Doesn't the fact that they took Daniel's computer make you think that they might be interested in whatever information you might have about his E-mail accounts?"

Audrey rolled her eyes at me. "GRrrrL isn't the one who tried to find someone to kill my mother. It was his faggot screen name 'boytoy2000' that did that."

She shouldn't have known about the ad Mooney had placed for the hired killer. I hadn't told her, it hadn't been in the papers, and there was no reason in the world for the police or the DA to give her that kind of information. There was only one way for her to know about the ad, only one possible reason for her to have that kind of information.

"And anyway, he didn't even hire someone to kill her. He did it himself, driving *her* car," she continued.

I sat there on the couch, next to Abigail Hathaway's teenage daughter, and felt sickened that what I had feared was actually true. She wasn't just GRrrrl; she was also the person who placed the ad on the bulletin board. And if she'd placed the ad, I could be sure that she was the person who killed Abigail.

I rested my hands on my belly and felt the little boy swimming in the warmth of my body. I wondered how it was possible to spend so much energy, love, and tenderness creating a creature who could one day hate you enough to kill you. I imagined Abigail Hathaway, stretched large with the shape of her daughter, dreaming a life for her just as I dreamed one for Isaac now and had for Ruby before him. Then I imagined Abigail's face as she was murdered. Did she see Audrey driving the car? At the moment of her death, did Abigail know that it was the baby she had borne and nurtured and, surely, loved who was bearing down on the accelerator pedal?

"Juliet?" Audrey said.

I couldn't answer.

"Juliet? Okay, fine, I'll tell the cops. Okay? Juliet?" Audrey's tone was now sweet and wheedling. I turned to her and felt strangely, absurdly unafraid of this violent child. I'd sat next to many violent criminals, people who'd done the same or even worse than Audrey, and never been afraid. My clients knew that they could trust me to have their interests at heart, and for that reason they never tried to hurt me. Never. So often I was the only one who saw the tough gang-banger put his head into his hands and cry for his mother. So often I was the shoulder the heroin-using bank robber leaned on while he confessed the horrors the white powder had wrought on his life. I was used to scared people who did scary things. I was used to them, and I wasn't afraid. I reached for the girl's hand.

"Honey, what happened? Tell me why you did it." Tears filled my eyes as I stared into hers. There had to be some reason, some hideous story of abuse and betrayal that would make sense of Audrey's horrifying deed.

The girl blanched and jerked her hand away from mine.

"What are you talking about?" She got up and walked quickly over to her mother's desk, turning away from me.

"Audrey, please, you can tell me about it. You can trust me" I begged to her back.

She spun around. "You think you know everything, don't you?" she screamed, suddenly and harshly.

"No, no, I don't. I know that something must have happened. You can tell me, Audrey. You can trust me. I care about you."

"You think it's so damn easy being Madame Perfect Mother's screwed-up daughter?" She was crying now, dry, hacking sobs that made her voice crack and break. Words poured from her in a torrent. "You all think that she was so great, but she wasn't. She was a nightmare! A nightmare! Nothing I ever did was good enough. Nothing! She loved every single one of those little brats in her school more than she ever loved me." She wiped at her nose, angrily, drawing a smear of tears and snot across her cheek. "I hated her!"

Whatever she had done, this child was in terrible pain. Whatever had made her do it, she really was nothing more than a poor, scared child.

I walked over to her, slowly, and reached my arms out for her. She fell against me, awkwardly because of the protrusion of my stomach, and rested her head on my shoulder. Sobbing heavily, she continued, "I hated her. So much. And she hated me. She did. I swear she did. They both did. They just hated me so much."

"Oh, honey." I stroked her hair.

"She married Daniel like fifteen minutes after my daddy died. She couldn't *wait* to marry him. And then they didn't want me. They never wanted me. Daniel used to hit me, you know that? He'd smack me and she'd stand right there and let him."

"It's going to be all right. I'll help you."

She stood up straight and looked at me in surprise.

"You will?"

"Of course I will. I'll call a really good lawyer right now. And I'll go with you to the police. There are a bunch of defenses we can use. We'll figure something out." I wasn't so sure that we could, but now wasn't the time to bring up my doubts about the abused-child defense.

Audrey looked at me, horror-struck. "What are you talking about? I'm not going to the police." She jerked away.

"You have to, Audrey. There's no other way. They'll figure it out somehow, and it'll be worse for you if they come to you instead of you going to them."

"I'm not going to the police!" She was screaming again, and her face had turned a deep, blotchy red.

"Honey, calm down. I know you're scared, but I'll be here. I promise I'll help you." I leaned over to her, reaching my arms out again.

Audrey looked at me, her face contorted with rage.

"No!" She screamed and ran around to the other side of the desk. Before I could follow, she wrenched open a drawer, the same one I had seen her close when I had first walked through the door. She reached in and took something out. For some reason, it took me a few seconds to realize what she was pointing at me. Maybe I couldn't figure out what it was because I just couldn't believe it. Her hand was shaking, and the little silver pistol jerked in her fist.

Before I even registered that she was holding a gun, I felt a thud in the side of my right thigh. I didn't hurt at first, but the force spun me around, and my leg collapsed under me. I fell to the ground. I did my best to break my fall, but I landed on my stomach, hard. Suddenly the pain in my thigh was unbearable, hot and sharp. My entire leg felt leaden and useless. I rolled onto my left side and, crying, tried to sit up. I felt like my leg was on fire and that, at the same time, it belonged to someone else—I couldn't make it move. I reached my hands down and covered what felt like the fiery center of the pain, and watched as blood seeped through my fingers. It looked thick and viscous, and I felt faint. I lay back down again, closing my eyes. I thought of Isaac and began to whimper. I reached my arms around my stomach, almost as if I were reassuring myself that he was still there.

"Juliet." Audrey's voice wasn't angry anymore, it was small and quiet, or maybe that was because it sounded far away to me, like I was standing at one end of a long tunnel and she was at the other. I opened my eyes. She stood over me.

"I didn't want to hurt you," she said. I saw that she was crying again.

"Okay," I murmured, terrified that she was going to shoot again, but unable to get up or even move.

"It's just your leg. It's not such a big deal."

"Okay." That seemed to be all I could say.

"I'm going to go away. You wait ten minutes and then you can go."

"Okay," I said again, but she had already run from the room. I lay there, listening, as Audrey ran around the house for a few minutes. I heard her pound up the stairs and then down, a moment or two later. Finally, the front door slammed and an automobile engine started up.

I closed my eyes again, repeating her words to myself. "It's just my leg. The baby is fine. It's just my leg. Isaac is fine." Then I felt a familiar tightening across my belly. The contraction seemed to go on forever. The combination of that familiar but nonetheless awful pain and the new and terrible one in my leg were too much for me to bear. I tried to breathe through the contraction like I'd been taught, but every time I felt myself climbing on top of it, the agony in my leg sent me crashing back down. I lay on the floor of Abigail Hathaway's living room, crying with great, racking sobs. Finally, the contraction ebbed and stopped. I gave another small moan, this time of relief. My relief was short-lived, however, because the ache in my leg started to overwhelm me again. I realized that I might not have a lot of time before the next contraction came. I couldn't stand much more of these competing agonies. Using every ounce of strength I could summon, and keeping before me the vision of baby Isaac desperately trying to get out of his wounded mother's body, I bent my left leg and rolled over onto my left side. Keeping as much of my weight on my hands as I could, I slowly began pushing up off the floor. Every movement of my right leg brought another wave of pain crashing over me. I kept it as still as I could, and slowly, impossibly slowly, I dragged myself, using my hands and my left leg and pulling my useless limb behind me, over to the couch where my purse lay. I reached up for my purse, grabbed it, and collapsed onto the floor next to the sofa. I dug frantically for my cell phone. Then I dialed 911 and waited. Nothing happened. I began crying again, this time in frustration, and only a minute later realized that I'd forgotten to press "send." I jammed my finger onto the button and, wonderfully, heard the sound of the ringing. I was on hold for a while, how long I don't know, because I had a contraction during the wait. I surfaced from the haze of pain to hear a voice.

"What is your emergency? What is your emergency?"

"Help me. I've been shot and I'm in labor."

"Are you having a baby, ma'am?"

"Yes, but I'm also shot. My leg. It's bleeding."

I felt another contraction coming impossibly quickly behind the last and had time only to tell the operator Abigail Hathaway's address before I had to put my head down and fall into the pain.

The contractions seemed to be coming one right on top

of another. After the next one, I held the phone in my shaking hand and dialed home. I began weeping with frustration when the answering machine picked up.

I have no idea what I said into the machine. I know I was hysterical with pain and fear, and I'm sure I absolutely terrified my husband. It was only after I'd hung up the phone that I realized that he would probably play the message in front of Ruby. I was crying too hard to call again. Hearing another hysterical message would only scare them more.

The wait for the ambulance was interminable. After a couple more contractions, during which I felt like I was drowning under waves of pain, I began dragging myself out of the living room and toward the front door. I turned once to look behind me at the beautiful Oriental runner in the hall and remembered how I'd been so afraid of ruining this same carpet that I'd cleaned up lasagna sauce with my shirt. Now I was leaving an indelible trail of blood.

I reached the front door just as the ambulance and police arrived. Reaching up to open it, I promptly collapsed into the arms of a man in a firefighter's black rubber coat. He had warm, brown eyes and sandy hair and looked exactly like the kind of person who could protect you from fires, earthquakes, and even homicidal teenagers. Holding me in his arms, he carefully eased me down onto the floor in the hall.

"Don't worry, ma'am. We're here. It's going to be all right."

I smiled at him and closed my eyes in relief. I felt another contraction begin, and barely noticed the police officers who were stepping over me and pounding into the house.

When I surfaced from the contraction, I found myself

lying on a stretcher, the leg of my tights torn off above my thigh, and my rescuer leaning over me, his hands pressing a bandage onto my wound. He smiled reassuringly, and I closed my eyes again.

"Ma'am. Ma'am," a voice said urgently.

I opened my eyes to see a police officer bent over me.

"Do you know who shot you, ma'am?" he asked.

I just had time before the next contraction to tell the officer that Audrey Hathaway was responsible for my injury. I asked him to call Detective Carswell and tell him that Audrey had confessed to murdering Abigail Hathaway. Another contraction hit as I finished, and I don't remember anything about his response.

The next thing I knew, I was rolling through a white hallway. I saw faces leaning over me and heard a woman's voice asking me, over and over again,

"Mrs. Applebaum? Can you hear me? How far along are you, Mrs. Applebaum? Can you hear me?"

"Thirty-six weeks," I said. "It's too soon. The baby's coming too soon."

"It's all right, Mrs. Applebaum, you'll be just fine. Can you remember your home phone number? What's your home phone number, Mrs. Applebaum?"

I told her the number and then felt them hoist me onto a bed. I felt a sharp sting in my left arm and then, blessedly, nothing for a little while.

I awoke to hear the sound of voices.

"The bullet went clean through, and we've cleaned and sewed the wounds. The bleeding has stopped, and I don't think there's any collateral damage we need to worry about. The question is, do we allow labor to proceed, or do we do a crash C-section right now?"

"I'd like to get the baby out as soon as possible. The monitor is showing unfocused contractions two to four

minutes apart. She's only two centimeters dilated. It
could be hours before this baby shows up, and I don't like
the idea of putting her through a long labor after the
trauma of a GSW."

"No, no reason to do that. Anyway, there's evidence of
a prior section, so we may as well go ahead with this
one."

"*No!*" I shouted.

The two doctors looked down at me in surprise. One
was an older woman and another a boy of about twelve.
At least that's what it looked like.

"I'm having a vaginal birth," I said. "Call my midwife,
Dorothy Horne. I'm having a VBAC."

They looked at me doubtfully. "Mrs. Applebaum,
you've just been shot. Our primary concern is your health
and that of your baby. You should not be going through
labor right now."

"Look, I've been doing goddamn prenatal Yoga for six
months so that I'd be in shape for a vaginal birth. I've
read every goddamn book on vaginal birth after cesarean
ever written. I'm not having a goddamn C-section. Anyway, I'm fine. I feel fine." And I did; I was in no pain.

"That's the lidocaine. We've given you a painkiller."

"It's working. So I can do this. Call my husband, call
my midwife, and get me to labor and delivery." With that,
I felt another contraction starting. The anesthetic had
taken the edge off the pain, and this contraction was
much more manageable. I breathed my way through it,
making an ostentatious show of my Lamaze competence
for the doctors who seemed so eager to cut me. They
watched me, then looked at one another.

"Take her up to L&D. Let them decide," the woman
said, snapping shut the medical chart she held and walking away.

Within minutes I found myself in an elevator and on my way to the maternity ward. I guess my gunshot precluded them from putting me in one of those lovely bedroomlike delivery rooms. I found myself in a decidedly medical setting, strapped to the fetal monitor, and watched over by two nurses and a doctor. The doctor was a man, about my age, who was going prematurely bald. He looked like a nice guy, like the kind of guy you'd want to be your doctor.

"We're going to prep you for a section, Mrs. Applebaum," he said in a soft but firm voice.

"I want a VBAC."

"I'm afraid a vaginal birth after cesarean isn't a good idea, given your injury."

"How long have I been here?"

He looked at my chart. "About two hours."

"Is the baby okay?" I asked.

"It's fine. The fetal monitor shows a nice, steady heartbeat."

"Is my leg okay?"

"Yes, it's fine. The bullet passed cleanly through, and both the entrance and exit wounds have been cleaned and stitched. You're on IV antibiotics now in case of infection."

"So if I'm fine, and the baby's fine, how come I can't at least wait until my husband and my midwife show up?"

The doctor looked down at me and finally smiled. "I'll tell you what. We'll put in an internal fetal monitor, and if the baby remains in good condition, we'll give you another hour before we do the surgery. That should give your husband time to get here." He patted me on the foot and turned to leave. At that moment, Peter rushed into the room. As soon as I saw him, I burst into hysterical tears.

Peter crossed the room in two huge steps, leaned over the bed, and scooped as much of me as he could reach into his arms. I couldn't seem to stop crying as I nestled my head into his chest. Suddenly I felt a hot flash as he inadvertently brushed against my right leg.

"Ow! My leg!" I hollered.

"Oh, no," he said, dropping me like a hot potato. "What hurts? What did I do? Oh, God, Juliet. What happened?" I could swear he was crying, too.

"It's just my leg. My thigh. She shot me. Audrey shot me." Then another contraction began and I couldn't speak anymore.

I surfaced to hear Peter slowly murmuring my name. I felt his fingers in my hair, gently rubbing my scalp.

"It's over," I said.

"I know," he whispered. "I can see it on the monitor."

"How did you find me?" I asked. "Where am I? This isn't Cedars Sinai." I'd planned on delivering my baby at the plush hospital to the stars.

"You're in Santa Monica Hospital," a voice interrupted. I turned to see a nurse dressed in pink surgical scrubs standing on the other side of the bed, fiddling with the monitor. "The anesthetist will be here in a moment to put in your epidural."

"I don't want an epidural," I said angrily. "I'm having natural childbirth." Just then another contraction hit me. In the middle of it I turned to the nurse and said through gritted teeth, "Get that goddamn doctor in here right now. I want that goddamn epidural right now."

She smiled and left the room. Within twenty minutes I had a tube the size of a single hair dripping blessed pain relief directly into my spine. It put me into the most wonderful, magical pain-free mood.

I turned to look at Peter and smiled.

"It's working," I said.

"Good." He smiled back.

"So now tell me how you found me."

Peter told me how he and Ruby had come home about an hour after I'd called. Ruby had gone straight to her room to find her Barbies, and, thankfully, had not heard my phone message. Peter had immediately called 911. The emergency operator directed him to the Santa Monica police dispatcher and from there to the fire department. Within fifteen minutes he had tracked me to Santa Monica Hospital.

"Where's Ruby?" I asked, suddenly worried.

"At Stacy's. That reminds me: Stacy and Lilly both left messages on the machine. Lilly said that there's a space for Ruby at Beth El preschool. And Stacy said that a colleague of hers at the agency sits on the board of a nursery school called Robin's Nest . . . or was it Bluebird's Nest? . . . something's nest. Anyway, a kid is moving to Europe or New York or somewhere and there's a space for Ruby for next year."

"Wow. Two schools. An embarrassment of riches," I said.

"Should we go visit them?" Peter asked.

"You know what?" I said. "Let's just toss a coin. I don't think I have the energy for more than that."

Peter smiled. "How 'bout we just send her to the Jewish school?"

"Really?" I asked. "That won't make you uncomfortable?"

"Please. Of course not," he said. "It'll be nice. I'll learn all about Hanukkah and . . . what's that one where you eat in the hut?"

"Succot."

"Yeah, all those holidays. It'll be great. I'll call the school tomorrow."

"Thanks, sweetie," I said. Meaning thanks for calling.

Thanks for letting Ruby go to a Jewish school. Thanks for finding me at the hospital. Thanks for marrying me.

"Let's call Stacy and let her know I'm okay. She's probably totally freaking out."

Peter picked up the phone. "What's her number?" he asked me. I told him and lay back on the bed, idly watching the fetal monitor.

"I'm having another contraction," I told him.

He put his hand over the receiver. "Can you feel it?"

"No. I can see it on the display."

"Hi. It's Peter," he said into the phone. "She's fine. Long story, but everything's fine now." He turned to me. "Do you have the energy to talk to Ruby?"

I grabbed the receiver out of his hand.

"Ruby? Rubes? Baby girl?"

"Hi, Mama." She sounded so tiny and sweet.

"Hi, honey."

"Are you in the hostible?"

"Yes. I'm in the hospital, having Isaac."

"Can I come, too?"

"Not right now, sweetie. But you can come tomorrow. How 'bout that?"

"Okay. Bye-bye."

"Wait! Ruby, wait!" But she was gone.

"She hung up on me," I said, handing the receiver to Peter.

The door swung open and Dorothy walked into the room, dressed in scrubs.

"Hello, folks," she said in her soft voice with its touch of East Texas twang.

"Hi." I said. "I've been shot."

She smiled at me and walked over to the fetal monitor. "So I hear."

She picked up the strip and looked at it carefully.

"I've been talking to the doctor."

"And?" Peter asked, obviously worried.

"And I think this birth's not going to be exactly what you had in mind," she said.

"No kidding," I answered.

"You know, Juliet, Peter, they never go exactly as we plan. Every birth is a surprise to me. Some more than others." She sat down next to me on the bed and took my good hand in hers. "I know how much you wanted a VBAC, but I'm afraid that's not the best idea right now."

"Why not?" I asked, close to tears. "I'm fine. I don't feel anything. My leg is fine. The baby's fine. Isn't he?"

"You've lost some blood, Juliet. Not a lot, but enough to make you weaker. Isaac's doing okay, but he's not as strong as we would like. You know I wouldn't be saying this if I didn't think it was for the best, but I think it's time to get Isaac out of you and into this world."

Peter and I looked at each other.

"Your call, sweetie," he said, and kissed me softly on the forehead.

"Okay," I said. "Let's do the surgery."

Nineteen

ONCE I'd agreed to the C-section, things went very quickly. I was shaved, swabbed with Betadine, and wheeled into the operating room in just a few minutes. Isaac Applebaum Wyeth made his entry into the world not long afterward. He was a little guy—only five pounds, four ounces—but considering that he was a full four weeks premature, the doctors were pretty happy about his size. They didn't even make him stay in the neonatal nursery that first night. They kept him for a few hours, but then let him come to my room. I don't remember much about the next couple of days. I was more tired than I'd ever been in my life, and when I wasn't nursing the baby, I was sound asleep. Luckily, Isaac was a quiet baby at first—he pretty much slept and ate for those first few days. He was probably stoned on all the various painkillers he was taking in through my breast milk, but I was just happy to be getting rest.

At some point, after the surgery, Detective Carswell

came by, carrying, strangely enough, a blue, stuffed alligator. He stood awkwardly in the doorway and said, to Peter, "This is for you. I mean, for the baby. Is she strong enough to talk?"

"I'm fine," I said. "They pumped me full of morphine and I'm feeling absolutely splendid. Itchy, but splendid." I scratched my arm. One of morphine's more unpleasant side effects is that it makes you feel like you've been attacked by hordes of mosquitoes. The pain relief was worth it, however.

"Can you tell me what happened?" he asked.

I told him the story of how Audrey had shot me.

"You know, when police officers are in their last trimester of pregnancy, we pull them off the street. We don't send them out to get themselves shot," Carswell said.

"Lucky pregnant police officers," I said, gingerly shifting my thigh.

Carswell snapped his notebook shut. "You are one difficult lady," he said.

"No kidding," Peter interrupted.

"I may be difficult, but if it weren't for me you'd still be looking for the driver who left the scene of an accident," I said.

"I'm sure we would have ultimately come to the correct conclusions," Carswell said, not sounding sure at all.

He paused.

"Thank you," he said, and leaned over to pat me on the foot. He missed, and stroked the bed instead, but hey, it's the thought that counts.

After he left, Peter asked me, "I wonder if they'll find Audrey."

"They will. They almost always do," I said, and shut my eyes.

I was right. Audrey was arrested after using her mother's credit card to fill up her tank at a gas station in Oakland. I considered getting in touch with her after her arrest, but something held me back. I don't know, maybe it was that she had lied to me, manipulated me, and shot me. But I asked a friend, a very good criminal defense lawyer, to call her, and Audrey ended up hiring him. Luckily for her, she wasn't tried as an adult, and was instead allowed to plead guilty in juvenile court. She was sentenced to spend the years until her twenty-fifth birthday in the custody of the California Youth Authority.

Daniel Mooney was released from jail and promptly brought an unsuccessful malicious-prosecution suit against the city of Los Angeles. I wasn't surprised to hear that he also ended up in protracted litigation with the trustees of Abigail Hathaway's estate. Seems he felt that since Audrey was barred by California law from benefiting from murdering her mother by inheriting her millions, all the money should go to him.

Strangely enough, while I never spoke to or saw him again, I did end up hearing from Nina Tiger. She E-mailed me more or less to say no hard feelings and to ask to hear my "side of the drama." She was writing a memoir about the Hathaway murder titled, quite grotesquely, I thought, *From the Loins of a Closed Mind*. I politely declined to participate. I've never seen the book in bookstores and am grateful that the publishing gods were wise enough to keep that particular family saga out of print. So far.

Peter and I weren't so lucky with Bruce LeCrone. Not long after the events surrounding the Hathaway murder, the studio executive ended up losing his job at Parnassus in the most Hollywood of fashions. He was phased out of his executive position, set up in a luxurious office suite on the studio's lot, and given a multimillion-dollar production deal. I like to think that his calling a pregnant woman a disgusting cow in front of two-thirds of the Hollywood establishment and the television cameras of *Entertainment Tonight* had something to do with it, but I doubt it. More likely it was the box office routs of Parnassus' last few pictures that did him in. Before he left the studio he did manage, however, to tank a project of Peter's that came across his desk. It didn't end up being that big a deal, however. Paramount optioned *Ninja Zombies* and it sat around in development for a while, earning Peter a nice chunk of change and the revilement of every parent watchdog group that got hold of the script.

On my second day in the hospital, Peter brought Ruby to visit me. Her eyes grew wide as she walked in and saw me lying in bed. At first she seemed scared to come near me, but, Ruby being Ruby, she soon got over her shyness and within a few minutes was curled up next to me in bed, describing all the things she'd done with Stacy and her kids over the past few days.

I'd had the nurses take Isaac to the nursery so I could be with Ruby alone for a bit, but they soon brought him back for a feed. Ruby watched in uncharacteristic silence as the baby nursed. Finally, she turned to me and announced, derisively, "That baby is too little. He can't play anything."

Peter and I laughed. "That's true, Sweet Petunia," I said. "But you know what?"

"What?"

"He'll grow pretty soon, and I bet his most favorite thing to do will be to play games with his wonderful big sister."

"You mean me?"

"I mean you."

She looked at Isaac suspiciously.

"Okay, big sister," Peter interrupted. "Time to go home and let Mommy sleep."

"Okay," she said, and skipped over to plant a kiss on my cheek. "Bye-bye, Mommy."

"Bye, honey. I love you."

"I love you, too."

Peter bent down over the bed and softly kissed me on the lips.

"I'm proud of you, honey."

"For almost getting myself killed?" I asked.

"For figuring out that Audrey did it, for *not* getting yourself killed, and for giving birth to a wonderful baby boy."

My eyes welled up with postpartum tears, and I kissed him back.

After they left, I lay thinking about Ruby for a while. It seemed to me that my ambivalence about being home with her had so overwhelmed me that I couldn't simply relax and enjoy her. I had left work to be with my child and ended up resenting her for it. Surely she already sensed this; how long would it be before she ended up mirroring it? While I was pretty sure that Ruby would never do anything like the awful thing that Audrey had done, I realized that I had, like Ebenezer Scrooge, been given a glimpse of Christmas future, and an opportunity to change things before it was too late. Isaac gave a squawk and I leaned over his bassinet, thinking that I was going to have to figure out some way to be a good mother without losing myself in the process. But first I was going to have to figure out a way to talk one of the nurses into changing that stinky diaper.